I0632671

The Toolbox

YVETTE WHITTINGTON

RopeSwing Press
an imprint of
Rope Swing Publishing

RopeSwing
Press

an imprint of
Rope Swing Publishing

This book is dedicated to my mother.
Your wisdom and infinite ability to guide
me and others has always been an inspiration
to me. In times when I needed you most you have
always been there. I listened to each "may I make
a suggestion," but truly only heard them when I
became an adult. I love you mom and
I hope I make you proud.

Vet

CONTENT WARNING

Prologue

H e stood six foot seven and made of steel.
Or so I and every other kid in the neighborhood believed. With just one look, before he opened his mouth, my dad could make you stop dead in your track, searching your soul for any wrong doing you had tucked away there.

He was a kind and honest man, a gentle giant some would say, and everyone who met him loved him. He would tell stories of his hunting expeditions, mostly tall tales, and soon he'd have the whole room listening intently. His smile was captivating; you always left his company knowing you were better for having known him.

My father, my protector and teacher, the strongest man I'd ever known would soon change the direction of my life profoundly through a grouping of seemingly unimportant objects.

As the sun peeked through my window and glistened off the dew-covered pane, I took a sip from the old, worn-out, coffee mug; it was still hard to digest all of the truths.

Chapter 1

In that tiny one bedroom apartment, I sat looking back on my life and was so thankful to be exactly where I was. It definitely wasn't how my life was supposed to go, but it was far better than it should've been.

Turning thirty really hit home, and with nothing better to do I sat on my couch unable to hold back the tears. My daughters, Nicole and Ann, were gone for the weekend with my mom. I had no plans; mostly to sit there and take a break.

I can still hear the mother next door, yelling at those sweet kids with the silky blond hair and pretty blue eyes. They were very timid when they first began coming over, but eventually made themselves at home, and would come often to play with the girls.

Nicole asked me one time, "Mom, why are they so dirty all the time?"

"I guess they like to play hard, Baby," was all I could think to say. But I had wondered the same thing then and many times since. The kids would show up at our house in the same clothes, day after day, and would be starving. I couldn't turn them away, even though it was hard enough to feed Nicole and Ann, still, I couldn't turn them away.

Some days I didn't eat, or I'd relegate myself to left overs if there were any. Worth it.

In addition to the lack of food and decaying appearance of our apartment, we all shared a bedroom. I placed two beds in the room, the girls took one and I the other. On cold nights, we all slept in the same one just to stay warm.

The mornings were rough. I got up at four so I could get across town to bring Nicole to school and Ann to daycare. So much had changed in their little lives that I just couldn't bear to move them from what was familiar, not yet. Luckily, they were able to sleep on the hour or so it took to drive across town.

I still love to watch them sleep, so peaceful, so

serene. Christmas time was soon approaching. Another worry, but still worth it. I didn't have extra money, things were tight already. For them, I knew I would find a way.

I had to.

The girls were only three and six. It was exhausting, to say the least, but I knew I'd do anything for them.

They were my everything.

Defeated was how I felt most days. But I always went back to that lovebug and knew it was really just the beginning. I knew I simply needed to work hard and save every dime I could to better our situation.

Houses don't build themselves.

My sister, Jean, had always been the strong, outspoken one. The one that no one would cross. She was probably the strongest woman I knew. She definitely got it from Mom and I found myself wishing many times that I'd had some of their strength during that time.

I spent the next few hours in tears, on my couch. I remember mostly that it was so cold. I must have dozed off at some point, thankfully. When I finally woke up, it was from shivering.

Cold can be so lonely.

I awoke with a headache, as I always did after a crying so hard. I could see the evidence of my breath in the cold air. Taking to myself of course, since there was no one else there to talk to.

Just me, alone in that apartment.

I knew it would be a long weekend without Nicole and Ann there to fill the empty space in the apartment and in my mind. I thought back over the last several months and how much my life had changed in such a short time. Even though I didn't seem to have enough money at times, the girls had everything they needed.

It had been six months since "that day." I imagine "That day" will likely be what I will always call it. The reality is, the broken me was just too far gone to see it until it was almost too late.

I experienced the most profound sense of independence and loss in that one half of a year.

But now... now I am reclaiming my life.

Chapter 2

I was pregnant when my father was first diagnosed with stage four lung cancer. He made the decision to spare me the worry during my pregnancy and asked that everyone respect that decision and he would tell me when he was ready. I remember the day he told me, it was one of those moments when the air in the room seemed to disappear and I couldn't catch my breath.

The "C" word, especially in that time, brought to mind only death. He reached over and took my shivering hands and placed them in his, wiping the tears that rolled down my cheek, reassuring me he would fight with all he had, and that he needed me to be okay. He didn't want me to worry about him; he wanted all of us to continue on with our lives as normal. But nothing was normal anymore, nothing was certain only that my father was about to fight a battle that would bring him to his knees and ultimately take his life.

His battle was long and grueling.

I watched as my dad, the strongest man I had ever known, become a shell of the man he once was. I remember looking at him standing in the kitchen, all of his hair was gone, down to his eyelashes and wondering how much more he could take. He was nothing more than skin and bones. He was barely able to walk across the kitchen. His feet would scoot, the strength to pick them up must have been too much. He no longer had a voice; his vocal cords were paralyzed. He would never talk again; nothing more than a faint whisper. The side effects of the chemotherapy and radiation treatments were brutal, but had the ability to keep him alive for a little longer. His hands that were once callous, were now the softest hands I had ever felt. I made sure to hold them often.

I looked at every line in those hardworking hands, every wrinkle, and every mark on his face. I studied the color of his eyes, the prettiest green eyes I have ever seen. Not to sound vain, they were a mirror of my own, but his had something extra. Something mine didn't have. I knew it wouldn't be long before I would have to rely on those memories of him. I could feel the time running out.

I will always wonder how it must have felt knowing his days were numbered. How many times had he gotten on his knees and begged for his life to be spared? Did he cry alone in his bedroom, that was now equipped with a hospital bed and portable machines for oxygen and morphine?

He never wanted to burden those he loved. He would smile and tell everyone he was fine, never letting on how unbearable the pain really was.

He lived in a small Mississippi town called Summit; I lived in a small town in Louisiana. I wasn't able to be there on a day to day basis, which broke every piece of my heart. I drove to see him on the weekends, and I did go on every one of them. It wasn't easy; I had a baby girl that wasn't allowed near him due to the vaccinations she received. It was shocking when I learned that the girls could have made him very sick. So I had to find a babysitter each time I went to visit him.

Seth, the father of my girls, was no help. To be honest, I was thankful. He was in such a drunken stupor most days that he was lucky to be able to take care of himself. Some days he didn't. I knew this all too well, but I could no longer be his keeper.

My father was slowly dying; I no longer cared what the repercussions were with Seth were. My heart and spirit were broken.

I made the drive to see my dad each weekend knowing one of those weekends would be my last with him. I did my best to bring things I knew or thought he could stomach which wasn't much. I even cooked for Patty, my step-mom, and froze it for later consumption, just so she wouldn't have to worry about cooking. Money was so tight, but somehow I found the extra. It was the least I could do under the circumstances; she was the one there every day and every night, left to tend to him on her own and work.

I would find out later that it could have been better, much better. Nevertheless, she did the best she could by him, I guess. Care, after all, seems to be relative to the person.

Just like despair...everyone sees it differently.

Chapter 3

I remember my last weekend visit to Dad's house; next would be to the hospital. He was lying on the couch with the oxygen cord stretched across the living room. His old coffee mug sat on the side table. He was weak and I was heartbroken. As soon as he saw the tears in my eyes, he smiled slightly. I tried my best not to cry in front of him, but it was nearly impossible sometimes because he never complained about the hand he was dealt. I did my best to not show pity or fear in my eyes. That day I couldn't hide it. I knew in my heart the end was drawing near.

"Come lay your head down. Everything is

going to be okay." He motioned me over to him, and patted his chest as he mouthed the words.

As I lay with my head on my dad's chest, he rubbed the back of my head to comfort me. He was comforting me, as he lay dying.

That was Dad.

I can still recall the rhythm of his heart as I listened intently. While I prayed that God would spare him and a miracle would come our way.

In those, the final days of my dad's life, I waited for that miracle.

When I left that day and headed home with a heavy heart, I rolled the windows down and cried so hard I could barely catch my breath. I remember begging God to please spare Dad's life.

I pleaded with God, "please don't take my father." I needed him. I wanted my girls to know him better.

The following week I convinced Jean to come with me to see Dad; by then he was already in the hospital with pneumonia. I knew it would be hard for her, since we all handle pain differently, but I also knew she needed to see him. I'll always be thankful that she decided to make the trip with me.

The ride home was almost in silence. I watched as my sister wiped the tears that continued to stream down her face. It had been some time since she had seen our dad and I knew his deteriorating condition must have taken her by surprise. I told her she needed to come, things weren't looking good. Her initial reaction, looking back, was an honest one. She simply didn't want to see him like that.

"You can't put it off," my reply was simple. That was likely a harsh, direct response, but someone had to say it. I knew there wouldn't be time in the future for her to be ready to see him. Who is ever ready anyway? I needed her to feel the sense of urgency. And I am so thankful that she did.

I handle grief as I guess the oldest child is expected to; I take control. I think of my siblings and I feel like I am their protector, even though anyone will tell you none of them needed protecting nearly as much as I did. I was the weak one of the bunch. Really, I just didn't want Jean to have any regrets and I knew she would. She would never have regained the part of herself that she'd lost by not going. Honestly, I needed that part of her. Selfish, yes. Still true. I sometimes think that he waited for her to come before letting go.

Life resumed and he survived that weekend. Monday morning I was back at work.

Around eight o'clock, I received a call from my Aunt Nan. "Come now," was all I heard.

Come now.

I had to make it there before he was gone. I stopped and picked up Jean. Mom followed closely behind. I don't remember much of the drive. I do know I had never driven so fast in my life, or since.

Tragedy kind of becomes a blur at some point. Once we entered the hospital, I saw all I needed to see on my aunt's face. I thought we were too late. I could feel someone tugging at my arm, motioning me on which way to go. I knew what was happening and I looked for an escape. There was a cold hospital room with the body of my dad, waiting for his family to assemble around the bed. I'm not sure if I walked or ran. I made it to another room down the hall, hoping no one was in it. There I was, back in one of those empty hospital rooms, taking shelter from the hurt. I found myself on the floor, cowered by a desk, rocking back and forth. I felt my aunt beside me, trying to comfort me.

My Aunt Nan was one of my most favorite people in the world; she loved me. She was a feisty little woman with smart whit and a sharp tongue. I lived with her, Dad's brother,

Uncle Rob, and my cousins, Todd and Marie for a while in my teen years, so I knew her well enough to know she wouldn't push me until I was ready. And I, in turn knew when I was ready she would be there with open arms.

My stepmother came in and all but demanded I go into the room and tell my father goodbye. It was not something I wanted to do and I was determined I wasn't going to. My aunt, in her special way took control and told Patty to leave the room.

My aunt stayed. After some time, I'm not exactly sure how long, I stood up walked down the hall and stood at the open door. There he was. I was so afraid to walk through the doorway. I wasn't ready to say goodbye. I remember most how peaceful he looked, as if he were asleep and would wake at any moment and look at me with that smile, reassure me everything will be fine.

I slowly walked to him and put my hand in his, and even though he had slipped into a coma, his hand was still as warm as it always had been. Still, I knew this was a memory I would never be able to shake. I regretted it immediately. I should've stayed in that room with my aunt. I leaned over and kissed my father on the forehead, turned and walked out the door.

I made my way to the hospital parking lot without even realizing it.

I would be lying if I told you I even remember that walk, because truth is I don't.

I only remember feeling this overwhelming sense of sadness. My mom walked up to me, tears in her eyes. I knew my parents' history was playing on her mind.

Months prior, when I had dropped her off at my dad's, we all knew it was their final goodbye. No one ever asked what they discussed, and she never told. I only remember watching as my mom and dad, years after their divorce, years of hurt and anger, pride and letdowns, stood on his front porch, hugging. It was the fourth and last time I would see my daddy cry. When my mom turned to make her way to the car, I watched the steady stream of tears flow down both of their faces. It burned a bittersweet memory onto my heart.

I knew what it meant for each of them.

Chapter 4

We all need the comfort of our mother's arms; no one's arms feel like hers, full of love and comfort when needed most. Not all moms were, like her I realized, but for the ones that were there was no one who could replace her. Mom sat with one of us on each side of her, with our head on her shoulder as we waited for our brothers, Warren and Clark, to arrive. At eighteen and twenty, the two boys were far too young to have to say goodbye to their dad. I was twenty-eight and Jean was twenty-six. It just didn't feel like it was supposed to happen that way. I watched as Warren and Clark walked toward us, and my heart broke all over again.

The phone calls between us all came to mind. Each time they went to see Dad they would call me, upset and stating that all Dad did was complain and drill them about the smallest things.

"I'm not going back," Warren said after one visit.

"You must, for Dad. Get over yourself," I replied, my patience had thinned.

"I'm not going back either and I mean it, Eve," Clark added.

"Dad may not be complaining to anyone about this death sentence for fear of laying a burden on us, the people he loves, but he is mad, Warren. He is mad as hell that he has to leave us! He only wants to make sure he has done his job and raised good men."

How could I understand how hard it must be for the two of them, so young, as they watch their hero die a slow, painful death? Dad had taught them how to fish, hunt and be good providers. Then suddenly, they were expected to instantly be the grown men my dad would've wanted them to be. To remember all they were taught, and do it all without him there to guide them.

How much harder it must be for my dad to not know for certain he had done his job? Had he given both of them all the tools they needed to be those men?

Only time would prove that, something Dad didn't have.

Aunt Nan held a notebook in her hand and told us that Dad drew something not long before he went into the coma. It was a picture of a big buck.

In his last hours he drew a buck...that was so him. Hunting was his passion, as it was Warren's.

Looking a little closer I saw the faint signs of words in the top right hand corner of the notebook. It was barely there and had been marked through:

Meds, I need my meds
Please get my meds
Its time, he is here it won't be long
now.
Clark

Chapter 5

Dad taught me how to play softball. I remember hours and hours on the weekends pitching to his shop door with a strike zone that was unrealistic. His objective would become clear in time. After hours and hours of pitching, pushing myself to excel and trying to make him proud, it happened. I had finally pitched a hole in that old shed door. That's when he said okay, you're ready. I was confused at first, but then I realized in order to make that hole between that strike zone I had to hit it just right, and the hours spent pushing myself had paid off. I guess he was watching me as I studied the door, and I saw him smile and nod his head with approval.

That day was followed by several years of fond memories, softball games and tournaments. I never had a relief pitcher, not even once. Both my parents enjoyed being those parents, the ones that sat on the sidelines and argued with the umpire. Dad also coached a team my sister was on, so we spent a lot of time at the ballpark.

When we weren't pitching the tent and camping at property my dad owned in Mississippi, we were at the ball park on the weekends. The camping was the best times; the smell of bacon cooking on the Coleman stove, so many tents spread over the family land, it looked like a little tent city. Giggles circulating around from each of us in the night, hot dog roasts and s'mores. Memories you don't treasure when you are a kid, but hold dear to your heart as you get older. All of my dad's side of the family used to gather for Easter weekend on that property, but they were all gone except Aunt Nan and Uncle Rob. In all, it was a total of ninety breathtakingly beautiful, family-owned acres. The birds' songs seemed happier, the bugs less intrusive, and overall, the sun shone brighter there. Each portion had nicknames. The front half of the property, just along the main road, was Uncle Rob's and Aunt Nan's.

That's where they built their house to be close to Nana. Then there was Dad's half. He didn't want a boring name, he'd said, he wanted different ones. So one weekend we all came up with them together. The fishing hole, was where the large pond was located. Even though it belonged to Dad, he never stopped people in the area from fishing on it. He said if they could feed their families, then it is well used. Of course Clark hated that Dad let everybody fish there, because he loved to fish too and he was worried the pond would one day run out of fish. It never did. The campground was the portion of the property that Nana's house was on. We'd pitch our tent back about an acre and have campfires with roasted hot dogs and marshmallows. The woods, self-explanatory, was where Dad and Warren would go hunting. I never really explored it too much. Too many scary stories about boars. Then there was the clearing, a large open field full of flowers and sunlight. When Jean disappeared on the weekends, we always knew she'd be there lying in the tall grass, sometimes sleeping. Dad joked that she was just trying to get out of work.

During one of those family gatherings, the kids decided to play hide and seek, with only one problem. I was afraid of the dark. Truth is,

I was scared of everything. Santa Claus even scared me. My dad decided to partner with me because he knew I wouldn't play otherwise. The countdown began, and the perimeters had been set. Nana's old house was base. Even though it had been empty since she died, Dad still kept the lights on. He just couldn't bear to stay there. He said he thought camping on the back acres was much more interactive and fun for the family, anyway. Mom disagreed heavily, but she still had fun with us.

Once it was time to hide, Dad grabbed my hand and we took off, almost complete darkness lurked everywhere. We found a spot, sat and wait. Complete silence, all of a sudden I felt something move across my shoe and I screamed bloody murder. My dad got so disoriented he grabbed me, lifted me up and started running. Not realizing we were closer to the pond than we knew, within seconds we were in the water.

That set off a whole new line of frightening scenarios for my mind to wrestle with. I started crying, unable to stop. My legs and my arms wouldn't move. My dad was trying desperately to pull me to the levee, but I wouldn't let him. Before I knew it, all my cousins, aunts and uncles were standing at the side of the pond, watching us. I looked around, and in the bare light of the moon I realized the water was about two feet deep. My dad was standing looking down at me. After all that, Dad offered his hand and helped me out of the water.

He and everyone else were laughing at this point. I buried my head in his shoulder and he carried me to the tent. Once in dry clothes, I found Dad. He was whistling as he made S'mores.

Dad looked at me and winked, "You know Eve, it is okay to be scared, but don't let the fear paralyze you to the point of not living. Sometimes, our minds are our worst enemy, Sweetie."

We ate our S'mores while the others continued their game. We listened to the echo around us, the hollering and laughter. We laughed along with them when someone was found.

My dad didn't dare ask if I wanted to play again. The last thing he said about it was that he should've brought a flashlight.

Chapter 6

Sitting in the living room at my Aunt Nan's and Uncle Rob's house with all the family surrounding us, including Mom, who refused to leave our side, was comforting. Her duty as mother had been bumped up to security guard. I would imagine being the only parent left must've been quite a big task.

If it was a burden to her, she never let on that it was.

Warren walked up to me and handed me a set of keys, "Dad had given these to me, but he didn't say what they were for."

I looked at them and drew a blank. It was an older rubber key ring with two keys on it, the kind you could find at gas stations during that time. I took them from Warren and looked closer. On the back, I could see where dad had scratched all four of our names.

Eve, Jean, Warren & Clark

After sitting there for a moment I looked at my siblings, who seemed just as perplexed as I was.

"Maybe these are for the old barn across the pond," I said.

I don't know why I thought that. Maybe I had seen the keys at some point in my life, but they weren't registering clearly. However, there was something vaguely familiar about them.

Dad's side of the property, of course. I remember the many weekends spent on that property. I can still see him in his hammock drinking coffee, his worn mug with steam rising from the top. I believe, looking back, my dad was never as happy anywhere else as he was there.

Many fond memories of my father live on that land. I felt closer to him just being there.

Overlooking the pond on a small hill, Dad had built a shed, although shed didn't quite fulfill how big it was. I think he called it that because it was nothing special; all of it was made from scraps. It was definitely full of junk, knowing Dad.

"Want to go look?" Warren asked.

"I do," Jean added quickly. She always was the most curious of us all.

I thought we should, too. If we didn't, we'd never know.

We hopped into Dad's old Ford and made our way across the pond. It was so dark that it felt creepy walking with only flashlights to check if the keys fit. I passed my flashlight to Jean and she held it steady while I worked the key into the old lock and opened the barn door.

Those times are the ones people talk about for the rest of their lives. Looking back, I think I felt it coming. We all hear stories over the years about just this sort of thing. Something that changes your life, something simple even.

A childhood best friend had an experience one day when she was a young child. She was about to kill herself. She went outside, took a deep breath, knowing it would be one of her last, and a bird flew right in front of her face. She said it seemed to be moving in slow motion, because as soon as it was directly in front of her, it turned its tiny little head toward her and hovered a moment. Doesn't seem possible really, unless maybe it was a hummingbird, but nonetheless she was marked by it. It was such a strong connection to life that she didn't kill herself. Something that simple changed her.

I've thought of that story several times throughout my life.

Thankfully, Warren's flashlight caught something briefly on the ground right in front of me, or I would have tripped over it.

"Wait, Jean, shine the light down here," I said.

As soon as we saw it, there was silence. We could see an old, worn, tarnished toolbox.

I bent down.

The second key.

One thing about my dad was that his love for his children overshadowed anything and everything else. I have to add also that he loved my mother... until his last breath.

I've only seen my father cry four times that I can recall. The first being when my grandmother, Hazel, his mother passed away.

I didn't hear the story until years later, that my father had been very sick as a child and nearly died. Those types of stories don't really get shared with kids. I guess adults worry over their mental state. Worry that kids might stress over death. I understand it because I'm just as protective over my daughters.

Yet death is real. It's certain.

When you are a young adult being told something like that for the first time, you wonder why you'd never heard it before. I even remember being somewhat offended that I hadn't been thought mature enough to hear it. Again, now that I am a mom I understand why they waited.

Dad was very ill and my grandmother, Hazel, whom we called Nana, had everyone leave the home so she could care for him and only him. For months it was just her and Dad. She told a story over the years of how he went into the hospital. Even the doctors had a grime prognosis. Nana always claimed that a single love bug transformed her fear into faith that God would pull Daddy out of his illness. The bond he shared with her was so tight that we knew a part of him had died when she passed.

She was an amazing person, and such a fun grandmother. My cousin, Marie, and I spent many weeks together at her house whenever possible. We'd all shuffle through the fields finding flowers and pressing them into old books. I know it is awful, destroying God's beautiful masterpiece just so we could selfishly enjoy its beauty longer. Especially once you realize they were actually not being enjoyed longer. They were relegated to lying, flattened in a dark, dusty book. It may have preserved a memory or two, but what good does it do to look back on a discolored flower? Anyway, Nana said it was more about the fun you have doing it, than it is about the product. That's what she taught me and Marie because that's what she was taught. I didn't think much about it then, sadly. For me, it was more about watching the child in Nana come out.

I remember also, Marie and me playing cards for hours. We were able to eat all the cookies we wanted. Nana always made the best cookies. She kept them in an old tin coffee can that sat on her counter and seemed to never have a bottom. Nana made sure it was always full for all her grandchildren. Sitting on the back porch with her and Marie, eating those cookies after picking flowers all morning, are some of my very best memories of Nana. The coffee's heat rising from her mug made me want to grow up quickly, just so I could have one of those cups of fresh coffee. I wanted to understand why people make that satisfying sound on their first sip. Nana could cook good country foods. I can still remember the taste of her rice and gravy.

Her passing was my first experience with death. I was nine I believe, maybe ten, and I remember the heartbreak like it was yesterday. I've learned, since that day, that the unpleasant smell of funeral homes are all the same. No matter where they are, what state, who dies, it doesn't matter. Doesn't change the odor. When I close my eyes, I can still picture the pink flowers around the coffin, and remember watching my dad that day, like he was a stranger. Dad didn't cry for much, so seeing it also made me cry. I'd only seen him cry once before.

The months after would lead to another of the few times I saw him cry. Dad had to leave, we were told, he was sick and needed to go away for a while to get better. I can still see his tall frame walking to the car, looking back at us four kids as if to say "I'm so sorry." I don't recall how long he was gone, a month maybe two, I just knew we couldn't see him while he was gone. We did talk to him here and there and each time he sounded sadder.

When he finally did come home, we could see he wasn't the same. In time, he got somewhat better. We got back into a routine like everyone does, and no one discussed what had happened. I didn't really think much about it after that.

Mom's and Dad's relationship seemed strained in the years that followed. Mom would get upset and leave in her car. Dad would sit in his chair full of worry, hoping she would come back safe. My parents never fought in front of us, but we knew. We were sent to my mother's parents, Alvin and Martha, better known as Pops and Gammie. It was always random, out-of-the-blue, so I assume looking back that they took this time to try and iron out their differences. Try as they might, they just couldn't do it. At one time we seemed like the perfect family: vacations, nice home, softball games, camping, and bonfires with all the neighborhood kids.

At one time.

My parents weren't able to mend what had been broken, and my dad moved out.

I remember watching him in the front yard load up his things. That was the third time I saw my dad cry.

Dad did his best not to let us see him break down.

He drove off, never to live in our family home again.

I was told recently by my Uncle Rob, my dad's brother, that my dad put up a tent on the family acres, across the pond from his own property. It was all he had. And he never took it down. The tent eventually rotted, and all that remained were the poles with a few pieces of dangling fabric.

I think often how sad that must have been for him. What else had he done in his moments of desperation and sadness? Knowing how much my father loved us four, I know it must have been so hard to move to another state, knowing you wouldn't see your children every day.

Mom and I had a rough patch during my teenage years. I had become very mouthy. I was forced to go live with my father during my senior year; I say forced because I didn't want to leave. I had a boyfriend and friends. I couldn't imagine living without either of them. Leaving Aaron and my best friends, sisters Rose and Megan, would be torture.

I didn't like change, so the move to a new town, with a new school was terrifying. I didn't make friends easily either. I was quiet, insecure. So to me, that was the worst possible thing that could happen, especially during that time.

Chapter 7

It didn't take long for my boyfriend to figure out a long-distance relationship just wouldn't work for him. It really was for the best, but at the time I couldn't see that. My heart was broken for so many reasons. Rejection is like that...it leaves its mark and cast a shadow on the weak. Each time I felt spurned, all those feelings came back.

I talked to Rose and Megan a lot at first, but then slowly it was harder and harder to find the time. They wanted to come see me, but that didn't happen either. I spent most days crying in my room with the door shut. I remember watching my dad put one of his pistols above a shelf in his room days prior, and after one particularly rough day, with despair overwhelming me and nothing left to look forward to, I grabbed the gun and went back into my room. My dad didn't pay much mind about the hermit I had become, but something about this day must have alarmed him. I heard a faint knock on my door.

"Go away, Dad. I just want to be alone."

"I need you to open the door, Eve," he insisted.

"No, I just want to be alone," I said.

I heard him walk away and I was suddenly filled with mixed emotions. I was thankful he'd left, but I was also sad that he left. I looked down at the gun in my lap, and as more tears filled my eyes, the gun became a blur.

A knock on the door brought me back to the present, "Eve, open the door now!"

"I don't want to Dad, please just leave me alone."

"Eve, open this door. We need to talk, honey," They were more than words. He pleaded with me desperately. I remember the way his voice cracked.

I started crying, contemplating my next move. My thoughts kept going back to the sound of his voice.

I opened the door to find my dad, my sweet dad, down on his knees with tears rolling down his face. He grabbed me and hugged me tighter than anyone had ever hugged me before. I collapsed into his arms, until I couldn't cry anymore. There was nothing ever said about the gun, but I could feel him reaching behind me as I sat there in his arms. I guess that is when he removed it. When he left the room, it was no longer there. After that day, it was also no longer where he had kept it to begin with. I know he put it where it couldn't be found.

The days were so hard, moving to a new school, where I was most definitely the oddball. I wasn't a country girl and never planned to be. The girls did not like me at all, with the exception of one, Diana. She became a friend. The one I needed. She helped me through much more than she'd ever know.

I had no trouble catching the attention of the guys at school, which may have been why so many of the girls didn't like me. Two of the guys stuck out to me for different reasons. One, Kevin, was simply friendly. He had a girlfriend who didn't seem nice, but he was. Another guy, Toby, pursued me continuously. I eventually gave into him and decided to take him up on his offer to go on a date.

I was the envy of most every girl, according to Diana. They didn't know, but I wouldn't be for long.

Of course, Toby was the star quarterback; isn't that the way most of these stories go? His family owned several businesses in town, and they were very well known, as I was told, not that I cared much. I was just looking for love. Someone to validate me at a time when I didn't believe in myself.

And Toby could likely smell my insecurities a mile away.

~ ~ ~

"Did you ever think shop could be so much fun?" Kevin asked.

"Definitely not," I said.

"I make it more fun, right?"

I laughed, "Yeah, especially looking at your lopsided flowerbox."

"Hey, I did that on purpose. Flowers aren't all the same, why should flowerboxes be? Besides, at least mine is nailed together already. Need help?"

"Yeah, okay," I added a little sass, "Not the way yours looks."

"Ouch." Keven moved a bit closer to me.

"Wanna know something?"

"What?" I asked skeptically.

"You actually make shop class more fun," he smiled.

I didn't know what to say to that. We had barely spoken, how could I have made it more fun?

"Seriously," he paused, "Tell me about where you lived before coming here."

I took a deep breath. *Which part?* I thought, *The part where I couldn't get along with my mom? Or the part where I missed my sister and brothers?*

"Well, I couldn't get along with my mom. I don't even know why, really. We just seemed to fight all the time. She changed after my parents got divorced. I guess that's pretty normal. She said I'd changed, which again, I guess is pretty normal."

I paused, but Kevin didn't speak.

"I really miss my sister and my brothers, too."

"I think that would be the worst part. Do you like it here, so far?"

"Yeah, I do. My dad's cool, so, yeah."

"And I'm cool." He shrugged his shoulder lightly against mine.

"I guess, you're pretty cool, too," I smiled.

"You know, if you have any anger, now is the time to get it out. Pound that nail into the box; it'll feel good."

I looked up at Kevin. It felt like it was my first time really seeing him. He was staring back at me and I felt an electric bolt pass through me. He shuddered a bit, so I know it passed through him, too.

"Okay, let's pound this thing," I said.

Once I started, I realized just how much anger I actually had in me because not only was my flowerbox lopsided too, it also had some serious integrity issues.

I knew I wouldn't be getting an A on that project, but it didn't matter, my anger got an A.

~ ~ ~

Diana and Kevin sat with me at lunch. It was weird because they didn't typically sit with me, together like that.

"You going? Is it true?" Diana asked the moment she put her tray on the table.

Kevin looked over at me and waited for the same answer.

"Yeah, I am. Saturday."

I could see Kevin tense up.

"I can't believe you; the big city girl is going

to spend her Saturday night driving up and down the same boring street for hours. Be careful. He moves fast, from what I hear, so be careful with him," she squealed a little.

I noticed Kevin tense again.

"Kevin," I asked, "do you and Amy go?"

"Yeah, we do. Guess we'll see you guys there." He stood up to leave. Just before he walked away though, he turned and waved to me. It was weird because it felt like a goodbye.

A last goodbye. For some odd reason, it stung a little too deep.

Chapter 8

The date started off very uneventful. We visited the local burger joint first. Unfortunately, because of the size of the town the only thing the teenagers had to do was "drag Donmoore." This is a street that they just drove up and down all night. They would meet in the burger joint parking lot, talk a little, then drag some more. It was strange, but when in Rome...

Toby suggested we go watch movies at an office his family had on some land. I was relieved. I had, had all I could take of the "dragging Donmoore." I recalled there being a shop and several pieces of equipment on the land, which was so far back in the woods, I would not have been able to find my way out. Off to one side, further in a wooded area there was a mobile home, which I soon realized was the office he had been referring to.

We entered the mobile home, and to the left I saw a small bedroom with a bed. No notable furniture, other than that. I didn't think much of it as he summoned me to the right. There was a small kitchen area and part-in and part-out of the kitchen was a table facing a TV. He proceeded to pick out a movie and put it in the VCR. He leaned over and kissed me. Kissing led to fondling, which I tried desperately to prevent. Everything happened so fast. I've heard so many comments throughout the years about other women like, "Why didn't you fight back" or "Why would you put yourself in that position?" and it disgusts me. You don't know what your reaction will be; but I know now that most assailants rely on the statistics that most women will cower or freeze.

He picked me up against my will and carried me into the tiny room. I remember him holding my wrist down, which was no hard task, given I barely weighed a hundred pounds. Next to the star quarterback, who had a daily regimen in the gym, I was no match for him.

"No!" I remember screaming.

Only he continued.

"Please stop! Please!" I could smell his cologne and his voice in my ear.

"All you Louisiana girls are sluts. I've heard about you!" he sputtered.

I closed my eyes because I could no longer fight him off, and so I went to another place in my mind. I don't know how long I zoned out, but when I finally regained my senses, I was lying on my back with my shirt pulled up and my pants were missing. I laid there listening. Where did he go? Is he still here? Is he coming back? What should I do? I'm sure, these are all the same questions many women have asked themselves through the years. I never imagined I would find myself completely defenseless. I can remember feeling so dirty, and ashamed. I wasn't the one who should carry that burden; he was the monster that took my security.

But I did.

As I sat up to pull my shirt down I felt the full effect of what he had done. I felt like I had been run over, everything hurt. I could see bite marks across my breast. One was so badly bitten the skin was broken.

How did I not feel that when he did it? I could see the bruises on my arms already starting to form. I could feel my legs shaking.

Another question.

Fear set in. I suddenly realized I had nowhere to run.

I needed to find a phone.

First, I had to find my jeans. I pulled my shirt down. I look from side to side for my pants, but they were nowhere to be found. I heard him laughing, as if someone just told him the funniest thing he had ever heard. I listened more intently from the door and it felt as if someone kicked me in the pit of my stomach. I heard him on the phone bragging.

"I got that Louisiana slut," he laughed again. No remorse whatsoever. As weird as it was to think, looking back, I just was hoping it wasn't Kevin he was talking to.

I saw my jeans lying half under the bed, between the sheet and the cold linoleum floor. I reached down to grab them and my legs almost gave out on me. They were still shaking. I slowly pulled my pants on, but in the middle of putting them on, I heard the floor squeak.

I was paralyzed. I couldn't move.

I felt his hand creep up my back, like a tiger looking for its prey. If I had to imagine what lying in a bed of snakes must feel like, as they writhe and slither across your skin this had to be close.

Everything in me wanted to run. Where would I go? I was so frightened and ashamed, I just needed to get out of this. Humiliating as it was, I started crying.

"Are you ready for more, Baby?" His eyes had the coldest glare to them. How had I never seen that in them before? I pushed him away as much as I could. He smirked at my efforts. Toby held my chin in his hand and forced me to kiss him. The once handsome young man that I had been happy to have his attention, had become the vilest creature I had ever seen.

"No!" I yelled, tears streaming down my face, "You, you raped me!"

He laughed "Do you, the Louisiana slut, really think anyone is going to believe you over me? You came here willingly. Girls like you are so easy," he exclaimed as he flipped his hand in the air, disgust written across his face. "No one will ever believe you didn't want it." He motioned his hands up and down in front of his body, "Look at me."

I fumbled buttoning my jeans.

"I'm not worried. Now, lay back down. I'm not done having my fun with you, yet."

"No!" I screamed louder.

"Oh, really? I think you will," he pushed me

face first onto the mattress and laughed. "We are so far back in the woods, you can holler walking down the road for the next 30 miles and no one would hear you. I also cut the phone cord, so bye-bye phone."

I cried harder. I felt on the verge of hysterics, then again, I froze.

"Make this easy or make it hard. To be honest I kind of like the fight, so it's your choice!"

I went to that place again. The place I think we all have that we go to when we need an escape from the world around us. I think now, looking back, that it's a place of disbelief mixed with a bit of disassociation.

I'd been in that place before.

The neighborhood boy's hands all over me, fondling me when I was younger. I remember not knowing what was happening. We were all friends playing ball. I felt a part of something good.

Then one day, that all changed.

A deep growl brought me back to the present. Toby had his hands moving at a rapid pace. His teeth. I felt his teeth this time. He made sure of it.

I screamed out in pain. He didn't want me in my safe place. He wanted me present.

I tried to remain silent because I knew he

took pleasure in it. I didn't want to give him any form of satisfaction, but that was impossible at times.

I don't know how many hours it went on. I know it felt like an eternity.

After, as he was pulling me toward his truck, he put his arm around my waist. Sweat was dripping down his forehead. He pushed me against the truck, looked me in the eye and reminded me again who he was. I let him feed his ego. There was nothing left to do anyway. He had taught me not to encourage more violence.

"We'll have to do this again. And again and again." It amazed me that he could think for one second I would be back. Even in my terrorized but numb state of mind, I remember feeling a giggle bubbling up. Instead, I just nodded and agreed to all the ridiculous things he was saying.

I just wanted to go home.

Before leaving, he reached around and grabbed my hand and slipped his class ring on my finger. I was in shock. It felt as if it was burning my hand, like I had just received a gift from the devil himself.

We drove for what felt like an hour or more, until I finally saw the porch light to my house. As soon as he stopped in the driveway, I didn't hear another word he said. I was only focused on how fast I could get to my porch. I quickly reached for the handle and he grabbed ahold of my wrist.

"Now, Eve," he gritted his teeth, the veins in his forehand protruding, "let's not distort what happened tonight. You wanted it just as much as I did. I was just having a little fun, no harm intended, as he winked. "If I were you I wouldn't misconstrue what actually happened he said through gritted teeth. Remember who I am in this town. You are a nobody; I can make you a somebody." He leaned and whispered in an animalistic tone. "Remember your place Ms. Louisiana." He brought his finger to his pursed lips and then placed it on my cheek.

I slung open the door, and in one swift motion I tore his ring off my finger and threw it in the bed of his truck.

When I reached the porch, I saw him make a move to step out. Please give me a reason to call my father out here, please.

Only he simply stood outside his truck and laughed.

Chapter 9

I could never let anyone know.

I felt so dirty, so violated, so useless.

I just needed to take a shower. I walked in and Dad was in his chair. He motions for me to come to him.

"Dad, I really don't feel good I need to go to the bathroom," I tell him. He didn't ask questions and let me go without a fuss.

I closed the door and let my back fall against the door. I slid down and laid my head on my knees. I silently sobbed so that Dad wouldn't hear. I don't know how long I sat there, but finally, I removed my clothes. I could smell him on me. Bile built up in the back of my throat and before I knew it, I was hanging over the toilet. My legs were shaking uncontrollably. I noticed the bruising inside my thighs. The bite marks were already bruised and bleeding.

I jumped in the shower, set the water as hot as I could stand it, and let it rain a steamy baptism over my bruised and battered body. I felt the stinging as the water hit my breasts. I scrubbed so hard with the soft washcloth, I left abrasions. I couldn't get him off of me. I still smelled his mixture of cologne and cheap beer.

The next day was Sunday. I was grateful. I knew I would not have made it a full day at school. That was put off at least another day.

Tomorrow, I thought.

I decided to take a walk on the long dirt road behind our house. It led to the main highway. I thought a lot about all that had happened in the last several months. My life had changed so much.

I found a tree stump and decided it was a good place to sit. I longed to be at home in Louisiana, with everything that was familiar. Movement in the field where the pipeline runs through our property caught my attention. I could see it was a doe with her fawn, grazing in the field. I sat there in awe of this beautiful creature. She never even looked over. Did she not see me? Then she turned toward me, stared for a moment and then went back to eating. She seemed content with my presence. I sat there for a long while just watching them, thinking of my friend and her story about the bird flying in front of her. I understood.

When I made it home, Dad was working on one of his projects and I was already making myself sick thinking about attending school tomorrow. Dad didn't seem suspicious, so I'm certain he didn't have any idea something was wrong. He casually asked about the date.

"It was okay Dad, just a date," I said. Then I went on about my way. If he knew the extent of what happened to me in that mobile home deep in the woods the night before, at the hands of that boy, he would kill him.

Without a doubt.

Chapter 10

Monday finally arrived, as I knew it would. I did not want to go to school and face him, or anyone for that matter. In order to not draw too much attention to myself and cause for alarm, I got dressed, gathered my books, and went to school. The ride there seemed to go by entirely too fast. I knew I wasn't ready for what the day had in store for me.

I looked forward to shop. Kevin always had a kind word and a listening ear. He just seemed to be such a nice guy. But I knew he had a girlfriend, so I hadn't gotten too close. I didn't need to give the girls at school another reason to dislike me. We passed funny drawings and cut up in shop, but that was as far as it went. He was good friends with Toby, part of the crowd, you know *the* crowd that thinks they are better than others.

I still don't know how, because he seemed nothing like them in my company. I have never seen that side of him, but I knew it was best to keep my distance.

Dad dropped me off, waved goodbye and I turned towards the school and began contemplating that I should run across the street to the hospital where my Aunt Nan worked, and spend the day hiding in a vacant room watching TV.

First hour I felt eyes on me. I wrote it off to my own paranoia, after looking around several times and finding no one staring back at me. Effects from Saturday nights incident, is what I reasoned to myself.

Second hour I knew people were looking at me and talking. I saw it, felt it. Diana would soon be there and I'd have an ally. I would feel a little more at ease, like I always did when she was around. I didn't make it any further than the door when I saw Diana motioning for me to go to the bathroom. I got a terrible feeling in the pit of my stomach.

It wouldn't be good.

"Eve, I know you and Toby went out Saturday night, but, but, well it's the talk of the school."

I quickly replied, "You know I did." I hung my head as if what happened was written across my face. Although not my shame to bare, I still felt dirty. That's something people don't discuss. You can still know it wasn't your fault. Still know you were a victim, but you still feel the shame. You still find reasons why you deserve the shame. You still find yourself relating to what it must have felt like for Hester Prynne, in the novel the Scarlet Letter.

The social shunning.

"What happened, Eve?" Diana asked.

"I don't really want to talk about it," I burst into tears.

Diana looked at me as if she already knew. "It's okay," she whispered. "I don't believe a word he says. He doesn't have the best reputation."

Had Toby done this before?

She told me the rumors were that I was ready, willing, and able. Toby told his group of friends, which included Kevin, that I all but begged him to take me. That I let him take me every way there was to be taken. I looked at her with tears burning the corners of my eyes.

"That is not true," I was looking for an escape, but there was nowhere to go.

"I'm sorry, I mean, I know he has a reputation, but I've never heard him talk about a girl like that before," Diana said sympathetically.

Then, I remembered my Aunt Nan at the hospital. I moved past Diana and before I knew it, I was in the lobby area with Aunt Nan in my sights behind the nurses' desk.

I didn't have to tell her what happened.

She comforted me, as she always had. She reassured me that when I was ready, she was there. I sat in the hospital lobby by the nurse's station for the rest of the day. She called the school and made up an excuse as to why I had to leave in such a hurry. Apparently, her being a nurse and my being "at the hospital" went a long way with the school.

My father never questioned my Aunt Nan. That was why I let her tell him I left school that day.

"All you have to say to him, is it is a female thing and the subject will be closed, Aunt Nan."

The next few days at school were torture. I saw the looks and heard the whispering. I checked out early nearly every day and made my way across the street to the hospital. My aunt knew I'd be there and never once made a fuss about it. She just gave me change for the drink and candy machine and set me up in an empty room.

Nice thing about the schools in Mississippi, I could check myself out and I did quite often that year.

I couldn't help but think about Kevin. Why did I care so much what he thought? I didn't really know him well, I kept my distance. He attempted to talk to me, but I ignored him. The shame of what Toby had told everyone stung most thinking Kevin might've believed him.

Friday came at last. I picked a table closest to the fence to eat my lunch. It was the farthest from everyone.

I looked up and saw Kevin walking toward me. I had a connection with him from the start. Not sure where it came from and I'd never let him know it, but nevertheless it was there. He sat across from me, far enough away to be comfortable, and asked me if I was okay.

"Yes, why wouldn't I be?" I said casually and looked away.

"Eve, I heard the talk about you and Toby. I'm not asking if it's true, because I'm certain there is more to the story than what is being said. I'm just here to ask if you are okay."

"Why are you so worried about what happened? I don't owe you or anyone an explanation. You are free to believe what you choose." I kept my head down.

I felt him move closer. His presence made me nervous, but in a good way. I felt his hand gently reach for my chin in an attempt to get me to look at him. I jerked away. Not sure if it was because I was thoroughly offended at being touched, or because I wasn't.

"Eve."

Something in the gentle way he said my name softened me. The second time he tried, I let him lift my face to him. I had no choice. As soon as I looked up at him, I could feel the tears swelling in the corners of my eyes. His eyes were so kind, but my shame was immense.

I felt that connection, so of course, I panicked. I grabbed my lunch and bag, stood, and immediately walked away as fast as I could. I couldn't let myself trust. Maybe this was a big joke and he was part of it.

Maybe I would soon hear a bunch of kids laughing. I didn't.

I felt him behind me, although he was keeping a safe distance. I went to the office. The secretary already knew I would be checking out, so she handed me the slip of paper to sign. Kevin stood by the front doors to the school, getting smaller as I left.

I wasn't far from the hospital when I felt a

tug on my elbow. I let out a bit of a scream and turned around. I don't know why I thought of Toby, but I did. He was the threat, still.

"What are you doing Kevin? Why are you following me?" I demanded.

"I couldn't just let you walk away Eve," he replied.

"Why, because you are such a good friend? You don't even know me!" I yelled.

"I am a good friend to you, you just don't know it yet."

"Oh, right, let me guess, all those rumors got you thinking, right? If I get closer maybe she'll let me do all those things to her!"

"No," he stated simply.

"Don't you have a girlfriend? If Amy finds out you left school to follow me, then I will have an entirely new set of problems. I can't take on anymore." I couldn't understand why he was there.

"I don't love Amy," he stated and it startled me.

"Then why are you with her?" I demanded answers again.

"Because, well, to be honest, I feel sorry for her. She threatens to kill herself if I leave her."

"That's sad," I felt sad, and then I felt angry, "Is that what you do to girls? You stay with them out of pity? I can tell you with certainty Kevin, I don't need your pity!"

"Good thing," he sounded a touch angry, "because you don't have it, but what you do have is my attention, like no one ever has. I...I... can't figure you out. Since the day you walked into that school, I have been fighting the urge to get close to you, to get to know you."

"What exactly do you want me to do about that, Kevin? I didn't ask for your attention and I don't particularly want it!" I could see a flash of hurt in his expression just before he turned stoic, "Please Kevin, go back to school, you don't want to get mixed up with me. I'm the school slut, remember?"

"Eve, don't say that. I know what he said isn't true." Kevin was so definitive that it drew me closer, "Don't say that again," he softened.

"How do you know it's not true, Kevin? How could you possibly know it's not true?"

"Because, I know. I can see it in your eyes," he paused, "I can see the hurt in your eyes."

"Goodbye, Kevin. I think it's best if you go back to school."

Amy approached so quickly I hadn't seen her coming. She had her arms crossed, not far from the both of us. It was apparent she was not happy.

"Kevin, please go, I don't need this."

"No, I'm not going anywhere." He didn't need to turn around to know she was there. "Amy, go back to school."

Instead, she walked directly toward us. It caught Kevin by surprise. Before I knew it, her hand swept the side of my cheek leaving a sting and not long after, a perfect hand print. I looked from one to the other, and turned to walk away.

"Eve, I'm so...I don't know-"

I interrupted him, "Do not talk to me, not now. Not ever again! I don't know you and you most certainly do not know me." I turned from him to Amy, "And maybe you should rethink your position on killing yourself over him; he doesn't really seem worth the trouble."

As soon as I said it I felt guilty, but I was angry. I didn't really know why I was so angry at him, but I was. Even though I knew I shouldn't have said it, the sting of my words was much harder on me than on him.

He'd never know it, though.

I walked to the hospital. When I made it close to the sliding entry doors, I saw Aunt Nan standing there, waiting. She had witnessed the entire thing. Being the person she is, she didn't say anything as she handed me an ice pack.

Off to another empty room I went.

Chapter 11

The weekends came and went. The dread always started late Sunday evenings.

How was I going to do this day after day, week after week?

There were still several months left of school, and the days were getting longer and longer.

I avoided Kevin in all three classes that I had with him. He looked lost and sad most days. I hoped he was okay, why I am not certain. I missed our interaction, even though it hadn't really been much. Besides him, Diana was the only other person I had ever really interacted with. Other than Toby, but I'd do just about anything to forget that.

I took a table closest to the fence, as I did every day. Same routine, making sure I distanced myself away from everyone at lunch. Some days Diana came and ate with me, but I knew she had many friends there and it was difficult for her.

That was, after all her hometown.

I couldn't expect her to abandon them to be with me. I still heard the whispers and felt as if every eye was on me all the time. I find myself looking for Kevin, and each time I found him our eyes locked. I quickly looked away, of course, but that connection seemed important somehow. I thought often, back to the day when he reached for my chin. He had been so gentle. I remembered how it felt when he touched me. It calmed everything that rages in my mind, momentarily. Then it made me mad because it felt so safe.

A group of girls approached me while I was caught in my thoughts. I was surrounded by Amy and her friends by the time it registered. One of them, I dubbed the monster, because I couldn't recall her name and she was the tallest girl in the school, grabbed my pony tail and pulled with enough force to make me wince. Another called me several explicit names. She made sure to add in a cuss word here and there for effect. I heard ear-piercing laughter just before I felt a gooey liquid drip down the back of my neck. I immediately reached up to touch it and realized it was embedded in my hair to the scalp. It look me a moment after drawing my hand back, to look at it and realize it was glue. It was humiliating.

They didn't know, of course, as a child I had an illness that prevented my hair from growing. It was only when I hit puberty that my hair started to fill in. In that moment, those memories of being teased as a child came flooding back. My hair had to be perfect no matter where I went. I was always adamant about it being fixed at all times.

Humiliation never gets easier.

I was unable to move; unable to process what had happened. I felt someone's hand on the small of my back leading me, for some odd reason I knew that it was Kevin. His kind caring touch once again was calming a storm.

Still, my disgrace was elevated.

I had no fight left in me. I was emotionally spent.

He never stopped at the school office. He kept his hand on the small of my back all the way to the hospital. He motioned me to a spot under a tree outside the hospital, but never let go of me. He sat next to me and I buried my head in his chest, and cried.

He never said a word. He just kept his hand softly placed on my back.

~ ~ ~

"I don't want your pity."

He looked down at my hands in my lap and back over at me with the most kind eyes. "Eve, I'm not sure who made you feel not good enough, but you are," he cocked his head to one side, "and yes, inside and out."

I wiped my eyes, a small smile formed.

"Eve, what I like the most about you is, you don't even know how beautiful you truly are!"

"That sounds negative, Kevin." I looked away not sure what else to say. No one has ever said I was beautiful. When I look in the mirror, all I see is broken. I see someone afraid of what others will say or think. I see many things, but beauty is not one of them. I looked just behind him and I saw two cokes sitting there.

He smiled, "Your aunt brought them out here for us. She's pretty cool. She never even said a word, but mouthed to me 'you take care of my girl.'"

"Yeah, she's the best," I agreed.

We sat under that tree for a while longer, talking about odd things, laughing about weird girls who put glue in other girls' hair. I wondered as I sat there, laughing and feeling at ease, if that was what normal felt like.

When it was time for me to go home, Kevin bent down and kissed my forehead and asked, "Sweet Eve, who did this to you? Toby? Is it only him or more?"

I looked away. It was somewhat odd for him to ask such a thing. *Why did he care anyway?*

"You don't have to tell me... It's okay, Sweetness, but I'm here. I'm not going anywhere, as long as you don't want me to."

Sweetness. It was strange, but for some reason it gave me such a warm feeling inside. Comfort. I wasn't quite sure what to say in return, so I told him thank you, stood up, and walked away. Confused over the feelings that he stirred inside me. He was easy to talk to, but I knew it wouldn't lead to anything more.

My Aunt Nan called my dad and asked if I could stay the night with them that night. He had been in one of his down moods lately and she didn't want him to see what had happened to my hair. Dad always took the hurts of his children personally, and would be so upset knowing someone had hurt me like that.

As a small child, when I had the issue with my hair, he was always my protector, always there. I don't really remember it, but Mom told me he didn't take kindly to stares or rude comments. He took control to protect me.

Too bad he couldn't do that at school, then and now.

My Aunt Nan and cousin, Marie, helped me get the glue out of my hair, without having to cut very much of it. It was a big mess, though. Marie, who had been away attending college, had come home to visit. She was mad as a hen. She wanted names and physical descriptions. I told her not to worry about it. The time would come, as it does for us all, when they would answer for what they'd done.

That night I lay in bed with Marie, on the second floor looking out of the window that overlooked the pond. Their house had charm. We had the windows opened, ignoring the fact that it was about forty degrees. To top it off, the box fan was blowing in our faces. We set the electric blanket on high and talked, the way we always had when we were together. I told her about Kevin.

"Wait, I know Kevin. He is Todd's friend?" she asked.

Todd was Marie's brother, and of course

my cousin, as well. Only Todd didn't go to my school, so how did he know Kevin? Marie saw the question on my face.

"Oh, they play baseball together. Kevin's been here many times to stay the night with Todd." I can't explain it, but it made my heart smile knowing he had been there. I wasn't sure why Kevin was so worried about my feelings. Next to the talks in shop, we hadn't really had much interaction, except of course today.

I lay there thinking of the day I'd had and eventually fell asleep.

Chapter 12

One night turned into two, then one week and another. Dad would come by and visit, but he wasn't handling things the best those days, so I knew with his own struggle, mine would be too much for him to handle. Marie dropped me off at school the next morning. I was on cloud nine that I'd had the chance to visit with her. I'd missed her since she'd been away at college. She was more like a sister than a cousin.

I made my way to first hour. I knew Kevin would be there. I didn't know what I should say. How was I supposed to act? But to my surprise, he wasn't there. In one way I felt sad because I was looking forward to seeing him, in another, relieved because I dreaded the awkwardness that surely would've been present.

I made it through the day, which fortunately was fairly uneventful. I was able to catch up with Diana and fill her in. She had been out of school for a week sick. I still couldn't bring myself to tell her what Toby had done to me. Maybe one day I would. Diana looked behind me.

"Well, I better be going, Eve," she said abruptly, "I'll catch up with you later tonight. Call me."

I felt a hand on the small of my lower back and I knew immediately who it was. I could smell his cologne, and the nausea swept over me with swiftness

Toby.

"So babe, I hear you and Kevin are getting pretty tight! I bet he wouldn't think so much of Ms. Evie if he knew what she had done with me not long ago."

"You are a disgusting pig, Toby," I elbowed him in the stomach, but he simply pulled me tighter.

He bent to whisper through my hair and disgustingly rhymed, "You are a dirty little Eve, let the men put it anywhere they please," he laughed.

I struggled to get free. "You know as well as I do that what you did to me was not my choice. You raped me," I said through the tears that fell down my cheeks. "You are disgus-"

Out of nowhere, Kevin was on top of Toby. Faster than anyone could count, Kevin was landing punch after punch to Tobys' body. It didn't take long before the coach separated them, and they were both brought to the office.

I stood there for a while, unable to move. Diana stood beside me. I had thought briefly that she'd abandoned me to Toby, but realized quickly that she went to get Kevin.

I waited for Kevin after school by, his truck. I could see him walking towards me. He wasn't happy. His face had areas of dried blood, some scratches here and there, and his shirt sleeve was basically hanging on by threads.

Maybe he wasn't happy I waited. I decided to leave, but before I got too far he was there with his arm around me.

"Where are you going?" Kevin asked.

"I... I didn't think you looked too happy that I was here waiting for you."

"It's not you Eve, I'm still mad at Toby. I couldn't control it any longer, when I heard what he said, Eve. I lost it and more importantly

I heard what you said. I know what he did to you."

"You know? How can you look at me knowing that?"

"Eve, that wasn't your fault."

He ushers me into his truck. He asked if it was okay if we went somewhere and talked.

"Can we go by the hospital and let my aunt know, because I'm staying with her for a while."

Aunt Nan readily agreed and asked if it was Kevin.

"Yes Aunt Nan, it is," I answered.

"Good, I don't mind at all, and Eve, he is a nice young man. I didn't have a chance to tell you the other night, but I know him very well. He has stayed at the house several times with Todd. You are in good hands."

I looked to Kevin, "Why didn't you tell me you knew my Aunt Nan and Todd?" I asked.

"I didn't think it was relevant," Kevin explained.

"Well, since you know the way to their house, you could drive me there and we could sit by the pond if you like."

"That's sounds good," Kevin said.

We spent several hours sitting by the pond, talking. Mostly it was him asking questions. I felt at ease with Kevin, not worried about being judged, and he made it very easy to like him. He held my hand from the moment we sat down, to the minute he got in his truck.

"Eve, can I kiss you? A real one," he asked.

I wasn't really sure I was ready for that, "I'd like to wait."

"I understand, I know you have been through a lot lately. It will happen when the time is right."

He placed a soft kiss on my hand and we continued talking for a while.

Kevin told me that he had broken up with Amy, which made how I felt about him less weird. I wasn't sure what to do with those feelings; I wasn't exactly sure what they were.

When the sun set, he had to leave, but I wanted him to stay. I wanted this moment to last a lifetime.

~ ~ ~

The following few months passed about the same. I spent them with Kevin after school and on the weekends, mostly at The Fishing Hole. Diana would come sometimes and we would occasionally make our way to the state park, just down the road. Soon, Diana, Kevin, Todd Marie and I were spending most of our time together after school and on the weekends.

The talk at school died down a lot, not totally, but enough to where I fell into a comfortable routine.

I enjoyed Kevin and my talks. The long walks on the trails at the park. There wasn't much to do in that small town, and dragging Donmoore wasn't an option.

It was so easy to feel safe with him. Weird to say, but it felt like home, a place I missed so much.

Summer came and with it deeper feelings surfaced for Kevin. I wanted to tell him I loved him, but it never felt like the right time. Each time I felt I was close to saying it, he seemed to get uncomfortable and I definitely didn't want to scare him off.

Diana and I got much closer. We five spent nearly every long, warm day of the summer together. We fished, had picnics, even roasted weenies one night. I was happy to see Todd smiling. He and Diana had become quite close, it was easy to see they were smitten with one other. I was worried Marie would feel like a fifth wheel, but she never let us know if she did. The weather was always nice, like most summers. We walked for miles through all ninety acres, but, we never really went into Nana's old house.

Diana was afraid, but we did sit on the front porch a lot.

"Hey, we need to bring lemonade or something next time," Marie suggested, "maybe sandwiches, too."

"That'd be fun. I'm always hungry," Todd said.

"You are always hungry, Brother," Marie replied.

"So Marie, tell us about college. What's it like?" I asked.

"Lonely."

We all sat there for a minute and said nothing. Of all the things we expected, it wasn't that.

"I wish it were as fun as I thought it would be," and she kicked a vine that had made its resting place on the porch. "I miss home so much. I wish I would've just gone to the community college and stayed here."

"Why not come back then?" Todd asked, "Mom misses you a lot. And well, I guess I do too, a little."

"Because I think I'd be letting her down, ya know?" Marie looked at her brother, "I can tell she wants more for me than this town. I like this town."

Diana took a cue from me and changed the

subject quickly, "Where is your Dad's house, Eve?"

"He's renting one in town. He always talks about wanting to build here eventually, but he never does anything about it."

"Why doesn't he just live here? This house just needs a good cleaning and some TLC."

"It was Uncle William's and my Dad's mom's house. We called her Nana. She was awesome. We have so many memories in this house, it's sad to see it now. Uncle William hasn't set foot in it since she died," Marie said.

"Oh, that's sad," Diana replied.

"Dad said he keeps the utilities on so it wouldn't rot, but it doesn't seem to have helped. One day it is supposed to be mine, but I don't think it's going to make it."

We all simply sat on that porch, staring off into the distance for a while.

It was sad. Dad was sad a lot.

I remember thinking how down Marie really did look. Before long we were on our next adventure. Aunt Nan had hidden some things for a scavenger hunt.

We had the best time tromping through the woods, walking on the banks of the pond, all the while making laughter echo through the property. I could almost see Nana sitting on her front porch peeling peas, singing. I know it has to delight her so much that this place is still alive and still brings so much joy to those she loves.

Chapter 13

The school year started and everybody was on to the next small town scandal. Amy moved on, too. Kevin wasn't upset that she was with someone else. I guess I would've been jealous if he had. She seemed happy and was less abrasive toward me.

It wasn't long before Toby had taken the wrong girl to his secluded property, a girl with a family much more powerful than his. Those types are like that, they don't stop. When the police went to the trailer and found the evidence, including another phone cord ripped from the wall, they knew they had him. Star quarterback or not, there was no hiding who he really was. It didn't take long for one girl after another to step forward with similar stories.

I didn't.

The senior prom finally came around. I had never been to prom or homecoming before. Not really sure why, just never had. Kevin asked me to go and I said yes. I almost regretted it the moment I did, though. I hadn't really had to face Toby or Amy and the other girls at school. Kevin made sure he was always at my side, as if it was his responsibility to protect me, and that he did. In some strange way, I depended on him to do it.

My aunt and Marie were so excited about the prom; we even went to a fashion show to find my dress. I couldn't wait for Kevin to see me in that dress.

I felt beautiful.

I danced around the room with my aunt, not knowing Kevin was standing in the doorway. She stopped, so I stopped and looked back and there he was, the most handsome vision I'd ever seen. He was perfection in my eyes. He didn't take his eyes off of me, even as he shook my father's hand. We bid everyone goodnight and he walked me to the truck. As he opened the door and helped me get in, which wasn't an easy task with so much dress to load, he smiled at me.

A smile so stunning I felt dizzy from it.

He stopped the truck at the end of the long dirt driveway, before pulling onto the main road, and looked over at me.

"Eve, you have always been the most beautiful girl I have ever seen in person, but tonight, Sweetness, I can't imagine there is anyone on earth as pretty as you are right this minute."

I felt embarrassed and put my head down.

He lifted my chin with one finger, "Don't look away or down, Sweetness, that's not anything to be ashamed or embarrassed of. It's the God's honest truth and I hope one day you'll see yourself as I see you."

"Okay," It was all I could muster. "Well, let's get this over with. I'm not looking forward to it, I must confess."

"Yes, I know," he said, "You just sit tight, Eve, we will be there in no time."

The Country Club of Fernwood, where the prom was being held, was much further than where Kevin pulled into. I knew where he was going, but I didn't understand why, really. The old white house, the one we knew well from the summer. The one I knew well my childhood. It had been several weeks since we'd been there, but it looked awful, like it had been years since I was there.

"Why...why are we here?" I started feeling apprehensive; I even felt a hint of fear. "This isn't the prom."

He looked at me, "Sweetness, oh but it is, it's your prom. No one else's. May I take your hand?" He helped me out of the truck and led me to the porch.

"But, Kev..."

"Shh... it's safe. I'm safe," he whispered.

"But wh—"

"Please Eve, just trust me Sweetness. I promise I won't hurt you. Your Aunt Nan and Marie helped me decorate it."

I was immediately put at ease.

Nana's old house. It had only been six years since she passed. When she left it to Dad she must've really thought he'd live there. Everyone knew the house had been vacant since she died. I hadn't really thought about it much. I felt like Uncle Rob, must have kept it up a little through the years in hopes Dad would stay, because it should've been much worse. But by the looks of it that night, he hadn't done so since the summer.

We walked up the porch and it creaked as we did. Eerie sounds filled the air. I saw a faint light flickering through the window.

He opened the door and there in the middle of the room was a tiny lamp. Beside it were some hand-picked daisies, from the grass just outside the house, that I saw on the way in. He reached for a single daisy and put it in my hair.

"For you, Sweetness!"

There was a cassette player playing music in the background, "Angel" by Aerosmith.

He took my hand and led me in a dance. It was the first one I'd ever had. He was good. I was a stumbling fool. Luckily, he didn't seem to notice.

When the music stopped, he looked down at me. I immediately looked away, mainly so that he didn't see the tears in my eyes. It was too late. He reached down and scooped me up in his arms in one quick motion.

"Don't cry Eve, I know this is foreign to you, but this is what you deserve, this and so much more. I want to be the one to share it with you, if you'll let me." He whispered in my ear, "I won't let anyone hurt you again."

And I can honestly say I believed him. I knew as long as he was by my side, no one could.

We spent hours there laughing and talking, he even had an ice chest with cokes in it and two pieces of blueberry pie. We sat and ate and drank, and nothing in the world mattered in that moment, but us.

He dropped me off and we said our goodbyes. I was glad to be staying with Aunt Nan and Uncle Rob, not because I didn't want to live with my dad, but mostly because Marie was there often.

~ ~ ~

I ran upstairs and Marie was waiting. I told her about the night and I could see she was just as excited as me.

"I've never known boys would do this kind of stuff," Marie said.

"I've never met anyone like him Marie, I think he was about to tell me he loved me," I exclaimed.

"Well, did he or didn't he?"

"He didn't, not in words anyway. I'm kind of scared, I guess. At one time Aaron supposedly loved me, but it didn't take him long to move on once I was forced to come live with Dad. That broke me; he was my first love and my first heartbreak."

I lay there contemplating if I should tell Marie what Toby had done to me. I didn't want her to tell Dad or Aunt Nan, no one for that matter. I had not told anyone about the rape. Kevin and Diana knew, but I hadn't told them. I felt like I could tell Marie. She had always been the one person I knew I could share my secrets with and they would be safe. I needed to tell someone, for me. Marie started to cry when I told her. Then she got angry.

"Eve, how could you keep that inside. It breaks my heart he put you through that. He needs to be held accountable for what he has done to you!"

"Please don't tell anyone," I pleaded with her, "I wouldn't be able to live with the shame if anyone found out, and besides who is going to believe me anyway? I'm an outsider, no one here knows me. Just let it go. Please Marie, I'm begging you don't say a word."

"Okay Eve," she conceded reluctantly, "I won't say a word. I can see how upset you are and I promise. It'll be our secret."

We lay there for a long time, just talking and laughing until we both eventually gave in and went to sleep. I loved Aunt Nan and Uncle Rob's creaky, old house, It always felt safe. It was cold in the winter, but there were always enough jogging suits lying around to keep an army warm. The worst part was mornings, because it was the coldest part. I hated getting out of the bed.

I knew I didn't have to get up, so I laid there a little longer. I couldn't wait to talk to Kevin. I needed to tell him what he meant to me. Take a chance.

I looked for my warm ups, threw on my socks and made a dash downstairs to the cold bathroom. I quickly turned on the electric heater and stood in front of it, waiting to defrost.

I could smell bacon frying in the kitchen. I knew it couldn't' be Aunt Nan, because she didn't cook. Curiously, I walked further to take a look and it was my Uncle Rob.

"Good morning, Lil' Eve." He never talked much. He was definitely a man of few words. My father's brother.

"Good morning. Something sure smells good"

"There's plenty; your aunt will be down soon. She was at the hospital late last night," he added.

I loved seeing Aunt Nan. She always made everything feel better. It may not have been better, but it felt that way. That was certainly enough for me. She came in and I could smell her ChapStick. She never went anywhere without it. I can still see her running it across her lips every few seconds. I swear it dried her lips out more than it helped. She reached to hug me. I always loved her hugs. I hugged her back, so tight.

"I love you, Aunt Nan," My nose started to tingle and I thought I might cry.

"Look at me Eve,"

"Yes ma'am?"

"You look different this morning; you are glowing, Sweetheart."

I blushed and turned away, "I guess I am Aunt Nan."

Soon, Marie joined us, and we ate and talked. You could always count on there being conversation, followed by lots of laughter. There was never a dull moment in that house.

After breakfast, I took a walk by the pond, just outside of Uncle Rob's and Aunt Nan's house. It was so pretty there. More importantly it was peaceful. I heard the door slam. That's when I saw my cousin, Todd, barge out of the house. He walked around to the barn and I could hear his darts hammering away against the old wooden wall. He usually only did that when something was wrong. Then I noticed Marie walking towards me. She had a very strange look on her face.

"Eve, Momma would like to talk to you, please."

"Is something wrong, I ask?" but of course I knew there was. That's the thing about moments like those. You know. You may reject the truth, but for those first few seconds, you know.

"Please Eve, just come see."

I walked into the kitchen and I saw Aunt Nan and Uncle Rob sitting at the table, both with worried looks on their faces. My first thought was that something was wrong with Dad, Warren, Clark or Jean, or even Mom.

My aunt took my hand in hers and began to explain that she received a phone call from Kevin's mother a few moments before. Kevin left here last night and was driving down Highway 55, when a deer ran out on the highway and struck his truck, causing him to lose control.

"He ran off the road and hit a tree," Uncle Rob said softly, "I'm sorry Eve. He was killed instantly."

I felt my knees give way instantly. My uncle was there to catch me.

"But, how...I don't...oh my God, please tell me this isn't true!" I pleaded with my aunt. She looked at me, unable to say what I needed to hear. I made it to the door before collapsing.

That just couldn't be true.

I pulled myself up and walked down the big

porch overlooking the pond. I'd always been scared of the boat, but fear wasn't present with that much pain. I unwound the rope and jumped in the small metal cradle. I used the oars to get me to the farthest side of the pond, out of reach and view of anyone. I knew Marie was watching me from the front porch, with Aunt Nan standing behind her. I also knew they would give me the time I needed, and be there when I returned ready to help me.

I lay down in the bottom of the boat and cried harder than I ever remember crying since.

After some time, I don't know how long, but I know the sun had gone down, I felt a slight tug on the boat. I sat up and found I had drifted back to the bank of the pond. Marie was standing there, arms wide open and I fell into them.

Chapter 14

I just needed to be alone. I started off early that next morning with a back pack full of supplies. I walked and walked until I'd reached The Fishing Hole. That was the indicator that I'd reached Dad's property. I sat for a while and thought about my life.

How had I gotten here?

I watched as a few frogs jumped around the pond. When the sun was overhead and I knew it had to be just about noon, I decided to go further. I took the trail through The Woods. It was always so dark, with trees canopying over each dirt path. The dark was comforting instead of scary, which in itself for me was always alarming. However, shutting down my senses wasn't foreign to me. I was getting pretty good at doing it, in times of crisis. I stood for a few minutes and soaked in the autonomy. I felt like nothing could touch me there in that moment. I moved on through The Clearing. The tall grass looked like fields of wheat from afar. I could see why Jean loved it there so much, growing up. The sun warmed me and I felt tired all of a sudden, in a cozy way. I finally made my way to The Campground. It brought back loads of memories from when we were kids.

When we had family days and weekend camping trips.

When Mom and Dad were still married.

When we were all happy.

Or rather when I was happy.

Eventually, I landed in front of Nana's house. The one Kevin brought me to just two nights before. I walked up the porch and through the front door. The candles were still sitting there on the floor. The black wick seemed appropriate. The absence of a flame.

I wandered through the main room to the back of the house. It was in such disrepair, even with the electricity having been kept on, it was a mess. I broke down again and cried. I lowered myself to the floor and let it all come out. Everything from Nana's death, to divorces, to fussing with Mom, to moving there. All the comfort I felt that day, was all an illusion. Because this place held much more pain, than it did comfort.

Toby.

Kevin.

It wasn't home anymore. It was a pillar of despair.

~ ~ ~

I made my way back to Aunt Nan's, where my family was waiting for me.

"I'm so sorry Eve, I wish I could fix this for you," Dad said in a soft voice.

"I know Daddy, I know." What else was I supposed to say?

He quickly realized there wasn't much else he could say. "I have to go to work, Sweetie, I'll call and check on you later. I love you!"

My mom called and I could hear that she was upset. She said that she was sending her love, and to let me know if I needed her she was only a phone call away.

I wished she was there with me. I knew she would've been, if she could've been. Only that just wasn't enough sometimes.

In the midst of my hurt, I remembered Todd. How hurt he must be to lose his best friend. He had known Kevin much longer than I had. I looked for him and found him in the barn, sitting on an old ice chest.

"Todd, I'm so sorry. I know Kevin was a good friend. This must be so hard for you." It helped, sharing that pain with him.

He shook his head and put it back down as if studying each blade of grass. I walked to him and gave him a hug, barely able to contain my own tears.

With nothing left to say, I turned to walk away. Then I felt him reach for me.

"Eve, he loved you. He loved everything about you. He...he wanted to tell you, but he said he kept chickening out."

That got me. I felt it vibrate throughout my body. "No need to worry about me, Todd. I never felt as safe and as loved as I did when I was with him." I walked away, although heartbroken, knowing he loved me and it gave me some comfort.

I made it through the night, even though I felt as if my heart was literally breaking in two. The next day was school. Aunt Nan told me I didn't have to go.

"No one will be mad or upset if you don't feel

like you can. If they do get upset, they'll have to deal with me," she added for effect.

I probably should have stayed, but I would've simply gone crazy there all day. Alone, thinking of him. And I needed to see Diana.

Diana never said a word; she simply grabbed and hugged me. I stood there for a long while crying, letting my heart be broken.

"I didn't tell him I loved him Diana. Kevin wanted to tell me, maybe if I had said it...I did love him, I do."

I didn't think after Aaron, that I would be able to love anyone else. It wasn't worth it. Aaron was my first love. It was powerful and real. I never thought I would be able to overcome it. I understood he had to move on. There was no way a long-distance relationship would've worked, but it didn't make it any easier no matter the reason. I realized the pain of loss is powerful, every time you experience it. It never gets easier; each loss takes a little more of you with it. It compiles over time and you think you would eventually become immune to it. But nothing could be further from the truth.

I made it through the rest of that day and knew the dreaded funeral would take place the next. I was expected to go, I knew, but I just couldn't. Death was so final, I'd much rather remember him yhe way he was that night, handsome and strong, kind and gentle. It felt as if he was handpicked especially for me, like my own personal angel. So, there was no way I was going to distort this beautiful soul with an image that I knew would haunt me the rest of my life.

Aunt Nan asked me when I got home, if I wanted her to come with me to the services tomorrow.

"Eve, you need to go honey, you need to have some closure."

"I just can't, Aunt Nan. I remember when Nana died and how sad Dad was. I remember what it did to him. This is hard enough. I don't want to remember him lying in a pine box. I'll keep his memory alive, the way I remember him."

"Okay Eve, but if you change your mind the offer still stands, Sweetie."

I chose to miss school the next day and I decided that I would visit the graveyard once the service was over. I went upstairs and the first thing that I saw was my prom dress. It had already been hung up and bagged. I unzipped it and sat there for a long time just replaying the night in my head. The dried-up daisy lying in the bottom of the bag caught my attention.

If I hadn't already been crying, that would've done it.

I must've fallen asleep. I awoke with the worst headache. I looked toward the clock and realized the funeral had long been over. The daisy was still in my hand. I decided to bring it where it belonged.

The drive over was long, and I wasn't certain exactly where his plot was. A town this small surely wouldn't have had too many deaths in one day. I pulled into the graveyard and drove around the winding driveway, looking for fresh dirt. It didn't take much to spot the most beautiful area off to the side under the prettiest, huge oak tree. The sun was shining down as if God himself had guided me to Kevin's resting place. There were flowers surrounding the hefty mound of dirt. I parked, the daisy still in hand.

Sad that my life was now down to a dried flower crumbling slightly in my grasp.

Making my way closer, I noticed a Ziplock bag lying on the mound, and written on the white spot that was made to house words like "fresh Green Beans – Jan 15th" or "Blueberries – picked Dec 20th" was my name in bold, black letters. I reached down, picked it up and looked around, confused.

I opened it slowly, feeling maybe it was a

cruel prank. Everyone in the town must've attended. There is no telling how many rumors were already spreading about the fact that I wasn't there. When I pulled out the folded piece of paper, I braced myself. It was a letter from Kevin's mom.

Dear Eve,

I know how hard it must be for you at this time; please know dear, Kevin cared for you. To be honest, he's cared for you since you used to come visit your father. I don't know if you remember meeting him at the town fair, but I think he asked your dad about you every time we saw him after that. I have never heard him so excited and inspired as he was when he talked of you. I understand that you couldn't make it today, but I knew if you were the exceptional young lady my son thought you were that you would come here, at some point. Eve, please do me one favor, never forget my wonderful son. Do not let this stop you from loving. Loss can do that to someone. Kevin would not have wanted that, he was such an unselfish person and because he loved you, I also love you sweetheart. I have enclosed a picture that Kevin had in his wallet of you thinking maybe you would like to have it. Thank you for making my son happy these last few months. Me and his father wish you nothing but love, happiness, and peace.

I opened the folded picture. He had taken the picture from the previous yearbook cut it out, and placed it in his wallet with a heart at the bottom. He had written (K+Y).

Was it possible for your heart to actually break multiple times at the same time? It has to be possible because at that moment I remember feeling as if it had. I laid the dried daisy at the head of the grave. When my hand grazed the cold dirt it startled me.

"I love you, Kevin."

The graveyard was very eerie. The headstone that had always given me chills as a child still stood tall across the field of cement markers. The headstone was a little girl in a wheelchair. I remember understanding in a weird way how heartbroken her mother must have been. She had died so young.

I left with no intention of ever returning. Like any graveyard, it was such a sad place. It's the same place where my own grandparents are buried. I had hoped that I would never have to go there again. Years later, life would bring me full circle to that cold lonely place, yet again saying goodbye to someone I love.

The rest of the school year flashed by in a blur. I did my best to keep my grades up, but in the end, fell short half a credit to graduate.

My English teacher advised me to come after school for the last two weeks, to makeup the half credit and get my diploma. I wouldn't be able to walk with the class, but at least I'd graduate. I agreed to do so. Unfortunately, the butterfly effect of life made its round to me that weekend, when my mom told me I could come back home.

Home.

The place I was expelled from will now be my escape.

I never thought twice about leaving that small town. I was ready to move home and be with my old friends again. Especially Rose and Megan. Feeling like I belonged. Lick my wounds, maybe. I'd have missed Diana, but she would've been leaving for college soon anyway.

Split decisions weren't good. They alter your life forever.

Chapter 15

I said my goodbyes to Aunt Nan and Marie, knowing both of them were unhappy with my choice. Knowing also they would support whatever decision I made.

I could see how upset my Dad was, and I hated to leave him the most. I knew Warren and Clark had decided to move in with him and would keep him busy. At least that's what I had convinced myself of. Also, Dad had met a woman and finally seemed content, and I was glad for him.

He would be fine.

"I love you, Eve. You always have a place here; take care of yourself and don't be a stranger," Dad said.

I made it to Mom's and the first person I saw was Jean, as she ran out to the car to meet me. I was so happy to see her, it had been so long.

Things were different between us.

It was sad and I knew in time that it would fix itself, but I needed her now, the old her. I needed the old me, too. We had been apart for well over a year and it would take time for us to find that place we once shared in each other's lives, and in our hearts as well.

I was able to go to my hometown high school graduation and see my friends graduate. I wished so badly that I could have been a part of their graduation, for that matter any graduation, but nevertheless it was so good to see them.

As time can do and did, it stole some of the relationships I had developed over the years. I almost felt as isolated as I had in Dad's town, not knowing anyone, with the exception of one or two friends.

I was reunited with the sisters, Rose and Megan. Rose was like a twin soul, we had a lot in common and we understood each other naturally. She had auburn hair and a fiery temper that rarely peeked out, but when it did, Megan and I went running. It was Rose's laugh that I missed the most, I realized once I'd heard it again. Megan was someone I looked up to because she had a cool confidence that was rare, especially at our age. She controlled a room the moment she entered it. Megan had the most beautiful long blond hair and thoughtful hazel eyes. She always knew how turn a negative into a positive, and for me that was never so easy. Everyone wondered how we three could click right back into the same friendship, but none of us had to wonder. I can still hear my mom say, "I understand you and Rose, but I don't know how you and Megan have remained such good friends over the years, because you two are such complete opposites."

Mom was right, but still I knew the bond I had with Rose and Megan was something that would last a lifetime.

Some friends are momentary friends, others are lifetime friends, and I had no doubts that Rose and Megan were lifetime friends. Rose was so funny and felt like a big sister, one Megan and I drove crazy sometimes. Megan's confidence and positive attitude balanced my insecure nature. I'd watch her sometimes in amazement and wish I could be more like her.

I was so glad to have them in my life again. Megan and Rose always felt like home.

Once I got a job, with Rose and Megan, of course, time seemed to fly past us and twenty approached quickly.

I spent the next year with them. We frequented the clubs at least three days a week. None of us drank alcohol, but we'd go to dance and have fun together. That is exactly what we did. We danced until we couldn't dance anymore. We laughed until our stomach's ached. And I soon found that my heartbreak of losing Kevin had eased to a small whisper every now and then. I wasn't interested in meeting anyone new and neither were Rose and Megan, so we went out week after week to have fun and simply live.

That's part of the danger, I know looking back. You tell yourself lies to make it. Lies like you don't want to meet anyone. Or that warning sign you feel can't possibly be the warning sign you think it is. How else would we cope through bad things?

I saw him across the bar. He kept pointing at me, so I danced a little closer to Rose and Megan. I was trying to divert his attention simply because I was not one who enjoyed being the center of anyone's attention. Most guys, once they saw Megan, lost it to her confidence and blonde locks. Only he kept looking and pointing at me. I decided to slip outside and get a breath of fresh air. It wasn't uncommon when one of us had to slip out for oxygen and a break every now and then from the crowd,

Lie one: *You aren't looking to meet anyone.*

I looked for the best escape route and I couldn't get out fast enough. I finally found a small balcony on the top floor. There wasn't much room, just enough to catch your breath. I suddenly felt someone standing next to me. I wanted to leave, move to another area, but he wouldn't allow it. When I looked up and saw it was the guy from across the bar, it startled me.

"Hi, I'm Seth," he said.

"Can you please excuse me, I need to get back to my friends," I said in a rushed whisper.

"Not yet," he said.

I felt warning signs, but I shrugged it off to my past with Toby.

"I'm not going to hurt you, Eve,"

Wait how did he know my name?

"Excuse me, but how do you know my name?" I asked, warning signs turned to alarm bells and they were ringing loudly.

"It seems you and your friends are regulars here," he leaned in to me, "according to the bartender. He said he knows all the beautiful women's names. Plus you are the only three ladies that drink coke and water every time you come," he smiled and it lit up his entire face. His eyes got nicer.

"So do you just go around asking about women everywhere you go?" I asked a bit disarmed.

"No ma'am, only the beautiful ones and you Honey are on the top of that list."

I felt him getting closer, and before I knew it he was kissing me. Hard. I had a horrible feeling in the pit of my stomach. I slapped him and reached around him for the door, but he grabbed my arm. It was faint, the anger. Surely I was mistaken. Right?

I knew what some men could be, but I also knew I shouldn't judge all men based on one.

Lie Two: *Danger can't possibly be the danger you think it is.*

Just then, when the alarm bells started to increase volume again, he apologized. He asked if I would stay and talk to him for a bit.

I don't know why, other than his trusting smile, but I agreed to stay.

That moment. That one, split decision, like many others, would cost me. I was warned by several instincts not to stay, only the lies we tell ourselves prevail sometimes.

I moved in with Seth only six months after I

met him at that bar. I was taken in by his love for me, his passion to have me. I didn't love him, not like I felt I should. I reasoned to myself that the time with Kevin broke me somehow. Kevin was so nice and gentle.

Seth seemed safe. He was also kind in his own way.

~ ~ ~

The first time it happened, I passed it off as him drinking, even maybe him not knowing what he was doing.

Another Lie.

It was Easter Sunday, he had spent most of the day watching movies and drinking with his friends. He told me earlier in the day to take time for myself, relax; so I did. I kept to myself in another room, reading and writing. When he came upstairs, I could tell immediately he was full of rage. He grabbed the book out of my hand and reached for my notepad. When he did, I yanked it back and before I knew it he was on me. One hand was around my throat, the other held one of my wrists down.

He forced himself on me. Once it was over I lay there, not quite sure what I should do. He was passed out and this was my chance to leave.

And I should have.

But the lies we tell ourselves get easier.

I heard the doorbell ring and I ran downstairs as fast as I could so it didn't wake him up. It was my mom; she had a huge Easter basket in her arms. I was in such a hurry to get to the door, I never even noticed my wrist was already bruising.

"Eve, what happened?" Mom exclaimed.

"I fell down the stairs last night Mom," I thought quickly on my feet. "It's pretty sore, but it looks worse than it really is. It'll be fine."

The lies we tell others, are sometimes the same lies we tell ourselves.

And my lies were piling up quickly.

Her visit was brief and I could see she was skeptical. The concern on her face was hard to miss. I'm sure I was able to convince her everything was fine before she left. I even believed it myself.

A mishap.

I'd faced someone who didn't care at all about me, when Toby had raped me. This was different. Seth cared for me.

It would never happen again.

He didn't know what he was doing.

I heard him call my name and knew I

couldn't face him yet. I remained downstairs. What had happened was not okay.

He made his way downstairs and I could see he had been crying.

He was sorry. Thank God.

"Baby, I'm so sorry for what I did," he fell to his knees in front of me. "Please forgive me, I love you. I would never hurt you."

I believed him. *Why would he hurt me intentionally?*

"You just make me so damn mad! Me and the boys had no food. I had to miss the movie to cook. Hell, the dishes are still stacked up in the sink. You couldn't even come down and say hello. You made them all feel unwelcome in my home. My home."

I guess somewhere in his apology I didn't really hear the words clearly, or maybe another lie to myself.

Looking back, he blamed me.

I forgave him and the days and weeks went on as if nothing happened that night. Things were so perfect then.

I would find myself, telling myself a lot of lies.

Chapter 16

I had lost most contact with friends. Rose went off to college and got a great job working with computers. Megan got married to her high school sweetheart and moved away with him.

Seth soon moved us to a small town across the river in the middle of nowhere. It was a small trailer park with cane fields surrounding us on all sides. I had never felt more alone and isolated.

I was secluded and away from everyone and everything I had ever known.

We couldn't afford a phone, he'd said.

When my car broke down, we couldn't afford to fix it. "It wasn't like I worked," he'd said.

He made sure he took advantage of my isolation. There were days at a time, that he would disappear and come home as if he had never been gone. I had no car, no phone, just me in that old trailer park with mostly empty trailers. I had nowhere to go and no one to call. I did make friends with a nice lady a few doors down; she became my saving grace at times. Ms. Faith was older, more my mother's age. We became secret friends. My father would come every now and then to visit, not much, but when he did I enjoyed those visits.

I never let on anything was wrong and Seth didn't dare show any signs in front of my father. I thought at the time it was because he was good. That Seth had good in him.

Another lie. It was because he knew better than to show that side, the real side, to my dad.

One week before Mardi Gras, Seth had left home and didn't return for two weeks. There was no food, nothing to drink and again no way for me to go anywhere. Luckily, Ms. Faith kept me fed.

Seth didn't know about Ms. Faith. *Surely he thought we had enough food for me to eat. He wouldn't have left me to starve.*

It was early morning. I'd heard a loud noise on the porch. I got scared and looked out of the curtains. It was Seth, barely able to walk, so he collapsed on the porch. I opened the door, didn't say a word. He starting cussing and hollering, asking me why I locked him out of his own damn house! I knew better than to engage in a conversation when he was this wasted, so I just asked him to please go lie down and we could talk about it in the morning.

He refused.

One thing I learned quickly, was that he was never too drunk to fight. It started with a slap. Always the open hand, simply because I think he was aware enough to know not to leave a lasting mark. When I ran from him, he chased me, grabbed my hair and forced me to sit down below him on the floor. He started to unbuckle his belt. I am not sure why I always referred to these confrontations as a fight, I guess it was easier than admitting I was such a coward. There was no fight, in order to fight both parties had to participate. I was never a participant, only a spectator.

"Don't just sit there, Stupid, I swear you get dumber by the day."

I went to that place, the one I was familiar with. The place I would rather live in; anywhere but where I was.

"You are going to make a choice: emergency

room or morgue? You have three seconds."

It took less than one. It wasn't a hard decision to make.

I didn't know these would become two words I would say often in my life.

Emergency room.

Emergency room

Emergency room

I think that day, maybe the lies started to crumble.

After the first round, he pulled me by my hair over to the refrigerator. He opened the door and the coolness hit my open wounds like another punch.

"Cook me breakfast. Maybe you can prove you're worth something." He stood behind me as I prepared the food to cook. Every now and then he'd poke me in the ribs, the ones I was sure he'd broken. The pain pierced through me like a knife.

He'd only laughed.

I stood at the stove afraid of the hot surface. Would he push my face into the open fire shooting from the old gas range? I hurried as fast as I could. He finally went and sat down at the table, barely standing on its own as well.

I felt a kinship with that table, in that moment.

That place again, to be honest I probably never really left it. Detachment seemed to be easier to face than finding the strength to leave. Only I didn't want to be detached. I thought of a sunset on the river like I used to watch with Megan and Rose. Humiliation ran through me, so I tried to cut that image off and go back to detachment.

What would they think of me if they saw me now?

Even when I tried to block out the reality of my life, it was there in every thought. Every sunset. Every memory, because it was all tainted by who I'd become.

As I turned around to bring him his plate, I caught the image of something, but it was too fast. The handle of the broom caught the side of my face and I thought my right eye had exploded. I ran outside on the porch. I could hear him behind me, felt the blows on my back, one after the other. I would've sworn it was more than one broom handle. I raised my arms to cover my face. It was all I could think to do.

I took cover on the ground, wailing. The blows had stopped, but I was afraid to look up.

Was he waiting for me to look up so he could once again take a shot at my head?

I heard commotion far enough away from

me, that I knew it was him. I looked up and he had disappeared into the trailer. Soon he reappeared with some of my belongings and threw them into the yard. I sat there in tears not sure what to do. I don't know how long it lasted, but by the time he was done my life was reduced to a pile of stuff on the ground. It reminded me of that mound of dirt in the graveyard; destined to consume me if I let it.

Finished.

I heard distant mumbling and looked around to find Ms. Faith in the yard, on her cordless phone.

All I could think was, please, God, please don't let her be calling the police.

I had nowhere to go. I desperately wanted to take shelter inside, to escape the shame and glares from the small crowd that had started to gather.

Seth came back outside and dropped a bucket on the ground in front of me. Soapy water jostled over the top.

"Get up and clean your mess. I want every filthy piece washed before you put it back in my house." He bent down and grabbed a hand full of hair at the top of my head, "And Eve, you better ring those clothes out real good so you don't track any water in my house." He looked at the sky, "I'd say sunset is about two hours off, you better get busy."

Then he let go of my hair abruptly and stood tall. I thought he was going to kick me in the face when he lifted his foot, but instead he rested it on my shoulder. "What are you doing old woman? Get back in your house before I have to come over there!" he screamed.

Ms. Faith. Oh no.

I didn't dare look. I kept my head down.

"That's right old lady."

Then he was gone. Back into the house.

I was almost done squeezing the water out of the last shirt to hang over the porch railing, when I heard the familiar sound of a diesel engine roaring down the gravel. Suddenly it slammed into park right in front of where I was standing.

As soon as I saw him, I broke down.

Daddy.

He was fuming. The veins in his neck were protruding. Recognition hit me and I looked toward Ms. Faith's trailer. Daddy held out his old handkerchief to me as he passed. "Wipe the blood off your mouth, then get in the truck, Eve. Now!" Then he raced up the steps,

I dabbed at the blood. It stung horribly and there was so much of it. A few minutes passed.

I was scared. What if Seth hurt my dad? His rage gave him so much power. I knew my dad was tough, but I definitely knew that Seth was, as well. It wasn't long before I saw the door bolt open. I opened the truck door to get out and just as I did, I saw Dad appear, holding Seth out by his neck.

Relief flooded me. I got back in the truck and closed the door. Seth had blood on his own face and down the front of his shirt.

I watched as Dad made Seth pick up all my belongings. Seth could barely stand. Seth did as he was told. Seth looked over at me, anger seething in his eyes, then my dad punched him another warning. I almost jumped out of the truck, but Dad saw and pointed at me. Seth loaded all of my stuff in the back of Dad's truck. When Dad started talking, I rolled down the window just a little. My dad, six feet tall, peered down over Seth, and moved slowly so that they were nose to nose.

"If you ever touch my little girl again, I will kill you. Do you understand me?"

"Yes, Yes, Sir."

Seth sounded so broken. He started sobbing. I jumped out the truck and ran over to them.

"Daddy, don't, please. It was my fault." He looked at me in disbelief. "Eve, I won't sit back and allow this. Get in my truck. You are coming with me!"

"Dad, I can't."

"You can, and will. Now move."

"I'm twenty years old. I'm not going anywhere. Seth was drunk; he won't remember what he has done once he sleeps if off. He doesn't mean it."

Another lie. I know it.

"Please Dad, I'm okay. You can go now. He's learned his lesson. I promise. I will be fine now. He won't ever touch me again. You taught him."

I could see Dad eyeing Seth. Seth nodded in agreement.

I knew, for fact, he would never hit me again. He knew now, Dad would kill him.

Seth really loved me. We had a few good times together when he wasn't drinking. I knew it would be okay now.

The next morning, the mornings after were always good, I woke up and all of my things were neatly put away. Seth was sorry.

It was those days I loved. Treasured. Those days were all I had to look forward to, but even then those were only temporary.

The truth among all the lies was the toxicity he created was what he then could save me from.

Chapter 17

I was so afraid of being alone.

When I found out I was pregnant with Nicole, I was overcome with joy. I knew without a doubt that would help him choose to be the better person I knew he could be. The one I saw in him occasionally. This baby would make him stop the beatings.

There were so many lies to myself.

I was five months pregnant when he left to go to a hunting club meeting. I knew that just meant they went to the local bar on the river and drank. Ms. Faith always took the hunting club meetings as an opportunity to bring me to the grocery store.

"I'll be right here waiting. You hurry. Wish I could give you more money."

"Ms. Faith, you do so much for me already. I just really need milk and maybe a loaf of bread. I won't be long."

I was standing on the bread aisle, looking for the cheapest one I could find, when a woman walked up to me, looked at my full tummy and said, "Girl, you Seth's wife? Yu got that man baby in your belly and he cheatin' on you, Honey!"

I felt like he was standing in front of me punching me in the face.

"I'm sorry. What?"

"You Seth's wife, right?" she asked.

"Um, well no. We aren't actually married. What is your name?" I asked.

"I'm Darla. Barmaid at the Red Dog Saloon."

"How, um how do you know who I am?"

"Oh, Seth showed us all pictures of you a while back. Told his buddies he had a real nice piece of...well, you know," she suddenly got uncomfortable. "I guess he was just braggin' on you is all. But Girl, I'd divorce him, you bein' pregnant with his baby. He didn't tell us that."

"What do you mean cheating?" I put my hands instinctively on my belly, "I don't think he would cheat on me."

"Honey, he cheatin' for sure. Been with a couple of us. I mean...the girls. Ya know?"

It was odd that she just stood there looking at me. Was she waiting for an answer. A reaction?

I left immediately. Ms. Faith didn't ask any questions when I got in the car and started crying. She let me cry all the way home.

"Come to my house later if you need to. I'll leave a key under the mat."

"No. He'd look there first. Thank you though."

"Eve-"

"I know, I know."

She dropped me off and I quickly stopped crying. I knew I had better have make-up on when he got home, so I rushed to reapply what I'd cried off.

The moment he walked in the door I saw the look. I rubbed the growing bump in hopes of reminding him. As soon as I looked down, I felt the hit. His fist hit my ear so hard, I heard ringing. I fell to the ground. I felt light headed and fought to stay conscious. I started to crawl toward the closet in our bedroom. It was the only door with a lock. He kicked me in the butt and caused me to lunge forward.

He laughed, "Always a klutz. If you were

pretty, it would make you worth it."

I stayed on the floor. I knew better than to try and get up. It was easier on me that way. After a few minutes, I heard him in the kitchen throwing stuff around, so I made my way as quickly as I could to the closet and locked the door.

He never came after me. I waited for hours, sitting, rocking myself, and crying for someone to save me, because I was too weak to save myself.

Seth came home the next day with a dozen roses and a candle. It was his new routine, to bring me something the day after. I had quite the collection of candles.

It got nearer to my due date, and I was hopeful. Things were going change.

~ ~ ~

My beautiful baby girl, Nicole, with a head full of black hair and the most beautiful eyes, came into the world and stole my heart.

The first weeks were very difficult. No sleep, trying to keep the house up and meals prepared was a full-time job. Keeping the peace was another full-time job.

I was losing hope, though.

Nicole didn't make him change; she only became competition for my attention.

I finally started to recognize the lies. I had to do something, so I decided to go on a job interview. We could use the money after all and he always complained about how lazy I was. That would help. I knew it. The local assessor's office was hiring and I thought it would be perfect. It was only two miles up the road and there was a small daycare in a house along the way. Putting Nicole in daycare was a little scary. I wasn't too sure about someone else taking as good a care of my child as me, but Ms. Faith knew both her and the assessor, so I was hopeful it might work.

I had it all figured out. I started planning. I scheduled my interview on the day Seth started a turnaround at the plant, because his hours would be long. Ms. Faith brought us to the day care and then my interview.

When I got the job, I felt something inside me shift. I didn't know what exactly, but I look back now and think it must've been that I felt I would have back-up maybe. Stability. Surely he wouldn't let me show up in his home town with bruises.

Again, the lies.

I waited until the day after, which had come

more frequently since Nicole was born. The day after he would be more receptive to my having a job. He'd let me work if I just stayed. So, on the day after with a puffy black eye and a busted lip I told him about the job.

And of course, he was fully supportive. I knew not to revel too much in that small victory, as the wind changes, so does his moods.

~ ~ ~

Nicole kept me up at night, so working proved to have its challenges. Ms. Carol at the day care said she'd help me get her on a good schedule, so she would sleep better. Before the first week was finished, Nicole had slept through her first full night and I was relieved.

I enjoyed my job. I started feeling a sense of self-worth that I had lost over the years. Seth didn't like it much, even though his dinner was never late to the table and he never had to take care of Nicole.

I was repeatedly accused of cheating on him. Thankfully the abuse slowed down, mainly because his drinking had slowed down. He still called me names. The tension started rising and I was fearful it would escalate his behavior. So much so, that I eventually stopped talking to anyone of the opposite sex, even in casual conversation, for fear he would misconstrue that and turn it against me.

Every man except my daddy.

I did my best to avoid confrontation with him.

Several months had passed and I felt hopeful. We'd had a lot of good days. It started slowly, minor slaps across the face, then his favorite slaps to my ears. He knew they didn't leave marks. One night in particular, I recall getting home from work, making sure supper was cooked and ready for him when he decided to come home.

When I heard his truck pull up, I started the microwave so his meal would be hot and ready. I had already put Nicole down to sleep so he could have a peaceful dinner. The moment I saw him, I knew it was not going to be a peaceful night.

He was drunk.

He walked up to me and grabbed me around the waist and pulled me next to him. The odor of alcohol floated off him like a steam boat. I hated that smell. He forced me to the floor by the hair. I was on all fours, and I thought he was going to tell me how dirty the floor was and make me lick it. It wouldn't be the first time he'd done that. However, it was much more sinister that night, so I went to that place in my mind. I completely detached any and all emotion. I never said a word, I did as I was told.

He was having trouble. He withdrew and yelled, "You are useless!"

Degraded.

I never said a word, but did as I was told. I didn't want to wake Nicole. I did my best to protect her from it all.

He left for a few minutes and then came back and continued the assault. When I cried out, he laughed. He yanked the hair at the back of my head so hard that my neck made a cracking sound,

Did he break it? Is this it? I'm going to die and no one will be here to protect Nicole.

Luckily, he hadn't broken my neck. Finally the assault came to an end. It likely took so long because he was drunk.

He stood up, kicked me, "Get supper now! I'm hungry," he demanded. "And clean the blood off the floor. Nobody can eat with all that staring him in the face."

I guess I made a face that he didn't quite like, because as I stood he pushed me into the wall so hard it left a hole in the drywall. Each time I walked down that hall after, it was a reminder of my life.

The next day was roses and candle day.

I hate roses. I hate the sight of them. I hate the smell.

I smiled though, and thanked him as I always did; inside I was repulsed.

I never believed the lies after that. I simply lived like I did.

Chapter 18

Two and a half years passed by on a rollercoaster. Seth would stop drinking for long periods and it was better. It wasn't ideal, because he still had anger issues and an obvious lack of respect for me in general. I often thought, who could blame him.

I guess what I wanted was for my love, or devotion to change him. Make him want to be a better man as my reward. I've seen men changed by love. Only not Seth. The reality moved from Seth being nurtured by my love and devotion, to simply being a devourer of it. He was a glutton.

The hole in the sheetrock, the reminder of

my life, had been repaired by some of Seth's friends. I was sad to see it go, because somehow it kept me honest with myself.

Hope springs eternal, until it doesn't anymore.

The abuse, when alcohol induced, was bad enough. But when it started to occur during his sober periods, that is when I realized, there's a chance I could lose my life, and if not my life my mind, even though at that time I do believe my mind had failed me already.

I wondered often, if I was destined to be this broken.

You can say you wouldn't put up with someone abusing you. You may even say people like me deserve it by staying. Unless you've ever been in it, you don't know.

Not really.

When Nicole was three she started asking "Where Daddy going?" or "Why Daddy gone?" I brushed it off and told her Daddy worked a lot to give us food and a house.

"He is here when he can be," I'd say often. Truth of it was, I loved it when he was gone. I no longer cared where he was, only when he returned.

I no longer worked at the Assessor's office. There was a co-worker that used to stop by daily, and it became a problem for Seth. The fact that he was able to keep tabs on me 24/7 was intimidating. I had no control over the amount of time the co-worker spent in our office, and to be honest I knew he had a crush on me, but I never encouraged it. He seemed drawn to me for some reason. I knew that there were no secrets in such a small town.

When I looked at him though, I imagined he was what Kevin would have been like had he lived. My life would have been so different had Kevin lived. I used to daydream about that and there were times I could tell Seth knew when my mind was somewhere else.

The one place he couldn't control, was my daydreams.

I found a new job in the city. Ms. Faith said I could use her car and I was so thankful. The drive was long, but a plus was that it was not just around the corner from our house. Seth couldn't ride by and keep tabs on me any time he wanted. I knew he did at times, but I also knew it wasn't every day like it had been. It was no longer convenient for him.

Nicole was the light of my life. I wish I could say I remember every little thing she did, but I don't. I do remember how smart she was. I remember Seth playing with her, the two of them laughing together. I remember thinking, how could he be that person in that moment, but the next, be the cold callous man I knew. I'd asked myself that question a lot through the years.

The playful times were few and far between. Nicole enjoyed those times so much. I would see the smile on her face, and how her big green eyes lit up when Seth would come home. Then the moment would pass, once he walked past her without a word of acknowledgement. It was heartbreaking.

Not long after starting my new job, I found out I was pregnant again. My dad had seemed different when we talked. I knew he had been really sick and just couldn't shake it, but I started to worry the longer it took for him to feel well. My dad didn't want me to worry. He was worried it would complicate my pregnancy.

Then, one day he couldn't hide it anymore. Dad had cancer and would have to undergo chemotherapy and radiation. I was devastated.

I had decided a month later that if my fate was to remain with Seth, I would not have any more children with him. I told my doctor that I wanted a tubal ligation once I had the baby.

It was my only choice.

The beatings started happening when he

was sober. I soon realized Seth was not a gentle man with a bad reaction to alcohol; he was a tiger waiting to pounce.

For so long, I went without speaking to my family, mainly because they didn't approve of Seth. He also kept me from them as much as he could, until eventually I found myself completely isolated from everyone.

That's how it happens. It's never a quick transition; it's a slow fade into the dark. If it were, many people wouldn't fall victim to it. I guess I've seen that people are strong, inherently, to survive. It's the wearing down that makes someone weaker and more vulnerable to the control of others.

So slowly, it is like the dripping of a faucet.

Drip. *Unfortunately we have to move out of the area. Get something more affordable so he wouldn't be working his fingers to the bone trying to pay for everything.*

Understandable.

Drip. *No phone calls after eight. He had to get plenty of sleep because he worked so hard.*

Understandable.

Drip. *No phone calls before he went to work. He wanted peace in his house before he went to work, since he worked so hard to pay for everything.*

Understandable.

Drip. *The phone bill was really getting high. No out-of-area calls because we couldn't afford it.*

Understandable.

Drip. *No phone. Don't need it anyway since we can't make out-of-area calls.*

Understandable.

It never occurs to you that each step the controller takes, is always one step closer to having full control over you. I believe it's not even necessarily a calculated act on the controller' s part; they don't have a pre-made list of Ways to Acquire Full Control Over Someone. Mostly, it is just one selfish act after another. Like courses in a dinner, that never gets completely satisfied.

Selfishness is never satisfied until it has everything for itself.

Chapter 19

Seth never participated in the excitement of giving gifts at Christmas, but he would hand me a fistfull of money and tell me to go get them whatever they wanted. I'd sit on the floor, putting together the toys and arranging everything so that it would be perfect for Nicole and Ann when they woke up.

"Keep the receipt so I can make sure you aren't stealing from me." I remember him saying more than once.

I wasn't allowed to buy anything for myself. Once I started working at the new job, he made sure that I never wore makeup, and dressed as homely as possible so as not to show off my figure.

I learned when Nicole was young after my cousin sent me some of her hand-me-down-clothes, that I couldn't wear whatever I wanted. I was so excited that I was going to finally get to wear something I liked. When Seth got home he was more than mad, he was infuriated. He called me horrible names.

Nothing new.

I eventually got used to the names, but at that time, it was devastating. He threatened to burn them all if I didn't give them back or give them away. I tucked them in our closet, intending to return them. A few months later I got home from the store and a huge fire was blazing in the back yard. He did it often to burn garbage, so I didn't think much of it. I went about putting the groceries away. I was leaning into the cabinet when I felt him up against me.

I smiled, thinking he was being affectionate.

He jerked me toward the back door. I was confused. Then, I saw all the clothes piled up by the fire.

"I told you to get rid of them!" he shouted close to my ear, "But you don't listen." The grip on my arm tightened and he nearly lifted me off the floor. I winced in pain. Nicole entered the room, Seth immediately let go and turned to Nicole.

"Sweetheart, will you get your daddy an ice cold beer so I can go finish burning the trash?" he said in his sweetest daddy voice.

Nicole, always excited when he was in a good mood, ran to the fridge and bounced back quickly.

"Here, Daddy," she held up the beer to him with the biggest smile on her face. He immediately calmed. I could feel the relief of tension that was so palpable.

I went back to unloading the groceries. When I was done I walked to the back door and cracked it open. He stood there, pouring lighter fluid onto the fire and adding a few pieces of firewood. He slowly turned toward me with a look that chilled me to the bone.

"Took you long enough. Lucky for you I kept the fire burning." He pointed to the clothes, "Get to it."

I walked down the stairs slowly. I know now, that was a defining moment; like that dripping of a faucet. There had been many drips up to that point, drips that led me down those steps.

As my foot touched the ground, I looked up and Seth had the coldest smirk on his face. Then, he blew me a kiss. It made my stomach turn.

He watched as one by one I threw the clothes, and my freedom, onto that fire. That surrender was not just a drip, it was a rushing firehose and I knew it.

Still, I did it.

I couldn't cry in front of the girls, so I retreated to the bathroom to compose myself. I could see Nicole's little hand under the door, reaching for my feet; she didn't like me to be too far from her. I opened the door and reached down to pick her up. Instant salve.

I was okay.

~ ~ ~

One Christmas in particular, I was pregnant with Ann, Nicole was almost three. I found an adorable doll house I knew Nicole would love, so I purchased it. It came in a million pieces, and putting it together took me hours. Seth sat in his chair cussing and berating me on how stupid I was and couldn't do anything, while he continued to drink without break.

I had just finished and was pleased I had finally gotten it done. I went to the back of the house to find my camera so I could take a picture of it. I heard Seth moving around. I was hoping he would fall asleep in his chair, like he had done so many times before.

He would get furious when he did and I didn't wake him up. Still, no matter the verbal abuse that came from letting him sleep there, I continued to do it. It was my only peace. It wasn't like when he was gone during the day and could show up at any moment. The reprieve from him being passed out was a sure thing. I would wake to him yanking the covers off, cussing, and sometimes he'd slap me a few times, but none of it compared to that peace.

Much needed peace.

As I walked back into the living room, his foot was hovered over the dollhouse, and the moment he saw me he plunged his heel into it. The dollhouse was hit dead center, causing it to shatter. He turned to me with that smirk, that smirk, and winked.

"Looks like you have some work to do, Darlin'."

I'd learned by then not to say a word. Be passive and let him do what he will. If not, it would only get worse for me. He walked past me barely able to keep himself upright, grabbed me, by the back of my head and forced me to kiss him. I hated the taste and smell of alcohol; it repulsed me. Everything about him repulsed me. Seth finally let go and went to bed. I looked at the dollhouse and knew I wasn't going to bed anytime soon.

I worked on the dollhouse for hours more. I finally sat on the couch, just to have some cushion and in my exhaustion, fell asleep.

I felt him before I saw him. The blanket we kept on the couch, that I fell asleep on top of, was yanked out from under me in one swift motion. I landed face down on the floor. Scared to move, I just lay there waiting for what I knew was coming.

"Get up, Stupid!"

He continued berating me. I rolled over and sat up. Before I could distance myself out of his reach, I felt the burn of the slap to my ear. He loved hitting me there. I balled up with my head to my knees and just begged him to stop.

"Please stop, Seth. Please. You are going to wake up Nicole." Those words had always been my saving grace.

"She needs to see how pathetic her mother is. I hope she wakes up and sees you."

I quickly got up for fear Nicole would come walking down the hall, and retreated to the bedroom where I knew I would be assaulted again.

His addiction to porn and sex had grown. It turned my stomach for him to touch me. There had been many times, when I went into the bathroom and vomited after his assaults.

He knew it, but didn't care.

I lay as close to the edge of the bed as I could without falling off. I spent many a night hugging the edge of the bed, as far away from him as I could possibly get. When he was completely wasted, he'd kick and fight in his sleep, sometimes leaving me with the occasional bloody nose.

The next morning I awoke to Nicole standing beside my bed.

"Mom, come see what Santa Claus brought me."

The excitement warmed my heart and reminded me why I endured what I did. I knew that on my own I would never be able provide for her like he did.

I had yet to learn that kids need quality not quantity.

Nicole was busy playing with all her gifts and laughing, saying, "Mom, look" every few seconds. When I heard Seth in the bedroom slamming drawers, I told Nicole to keep playing I would be right back. I made my way to the bedroom, not sure where I got the courage to do so, and asked as quietly as I could, what was wrong? The anger flashed across his face.

137

Sober and angry, he erupted.

"Come here and close the door," I hesitated and he said, "I will not ask again." As soon as the door is closed, he continued. "Are you stupid or lazy, Eve? Which is it? You don't know how to fold my clothes yet? You didn't iron my work clothes; you folded my sock into each other after I've told you time and again not to!"

I went to apologize, even though he'd never told me that about his socks, when he slapped me. His hand hit my face so hard I fell to the floor. Holding my face I looked up at him and I begged, "Please don't do this today. It's Christmas and Nicole is just in the other room waiting for me to come see her toys. Please don't do this Seth."

He walked by me and spit in the back of my hair.

"You are the most disgusting woman I think I have ever seen. Look at you. You don't do anything with yourself at all."

I sat for a moment, totally confused. I didn't dare say a word. I thought to myself, *you are pathetic Eve. If I had looked in the mirror, would I have even recognized myself anymore?*

I got accused of cheating if I fixed my hair or wore makeup. He wouldn't let me buy anything that he called revealing, but he would often tell me how pathetic I was for not taking care of myself.

I got up and made my way to the bathroom. I made sure to wipe any sign of the abuse off my face and splashed cold water to reduce the redness. I went back into the living room so I could try my best to sit and enjoy Nicole.

Seth walked into the room, and Nicole jumped up to show him some of her gifts. He never even looked at her. He walked out the door, cranked his new motorcycle and was gone. I was heartbroken for Nicole, but relieved. I knew my mom was having Christmas at her house, so I decided to go there for a little while to get out of the house. I let Nicole finish playing for a bit, then got us both dressed and headed to my mom's.

The car she had given me when she bought her new one was a blessing. Every now and then something went wrong with it, but Dad would always fix it and nearly dared Seth to say otherwise.

I hadn't seen my mom and the rest of the family in so long, I felt out of place. Mom kept pushing the hair out of my eyes, looking at me strangely.

"Eve, are you okay? We don't hear from you. Is that a bruise on the side of your cheek?"

"No, Mom, I have just been busy with work," I put my hand on my face, "and if there is a bruise, it is from Nicole. She was probably swinging one of her toys and it hit me by accident."

I saw the look in Mom's eyes. She didn't believe me, but she left the subject alone.

Nicole had fun playing with her cousins. She didn't really know them and I was glad she was having a chance to get to play with them. We said our goodbyes and my mom hugged me.

"Eve, you don't have to live that way, Honey," she whispered.

Although tears burned the corners of my eyes I never said a word.

We beat Seth home. I made sure to park in the exact spot the car was in when he left. I hurried in the door, in case he were to drive up.

After Nicole's bath, I started picking up the toys from the day. I thought of the joy in her eyes, so full of love and wonder, so innocent, so shielded from the hate in the world. I went into her room where she was playing, and gave her a little kiss on the head.

"Little girl, you are so silly. I don't know what I would do without you."

"You would be sad Mom. I mean you already are sad a lot, but you would be sad a lot more."

The words hit me like a ton of bricks. My sweet, three-year-old knew her mommy was sad a lot.

I knew I had to do better hiding it.

That night, I watched as she slept, so peacefully. I wish I could've kept her from ever being hurt. I realized that was what my mom was saying also. What she'd likely prayed over me when I was young.

I heard Seth outside. I didn't know how long he had been there. I prayed again, quickly, that he didn't know we'd left. I kissed Nicole again and turned on the TV in her room, just in case.

I made it to the living room, still no Seth. Maybe he had decided to stay outside for a while, I thought. I heard a strange noise and opened the front door. Seth was kneeling down in the dirt driveway by the back of my car.

"You thought I wouldn't find out didn't you, Eve?" he looked back at me.

"Find out what?"

"You brought my daughter with you, while you went whoring around. Tire tracks."

"I didn't go whoring around, Seth. We went to my mom's for Christmas."

"You are so stupid!"

"I wasn't gone long, Seth. I just wanted to see my family for a little while."

141

"You think I believe that? Where have you been? How stupid do you think I am, Eve? I have eyes everywhere. I thought you understood that."

"Well, whoever is telling you I was cheating is a liar."

"You calling me a liar?"

"No the pers--,"

"Shut up! Get inside and fix me something to eat. Then get ready for bed. I'm going to find out for sure if you were cheating. Then, I'm going to make sure you don't have a reason to cheat on me. Oh yeah Darlin', we are going to have some fun tonight! Just you and me, or I could always call the new neighbor, Liz from next door to join. Would you like that, Eve? No, I'm sure you wouldn't. Then you would have to see just how pathetic in bed you are. Especially beside her. Damn, I'd love to do her!"

I fixed his plate and retreated to the bedroom. I tried so desperately to go to that place, away from the torture and the hell. Only that night I just couldn't.

It was too real to escape.

I heard him get up from the table and make his way down the hall toward the bedroom. My legs were shaking and my heart was about to beat out of my chest. I pulled the covers up to my neck. I knew it could go on for hours. That night held more torment and torture than any night up to that point.

All done while he was stone cold sober.

The excuse that he was just a cruel drunk was no longer a viable excuse to justify the abuse.

I got out of bed the next morning in incredible pain. I could barely turn my legs around to stand up. I slowly made it into the bathroom and I wasn't prepared for what I saw. I had a pinkish colored bruise forming around my neck. My hair had been pulled so much, that as I stood brushing it, the sink quickly filled strand upon strand. My lips were swollen where he had bitten them, repeatedly. The inside of my thighs were bruised.

I heard him get up. I regained what very little composure I could. He walked up behind me in the bathroom, slapped my bottom.

"Thanks for a hell of a ride last night!"

I made my way to Nicole's room to find that she was still sleeping. Very unusual for her to still be sleeping so late. For a short time I stood there staring at her, how precious she was. She didn't deserve this life, I hid the abuse from her, but it was apparent that she saw how broken her mommy was. One day I would find the courage to leave, I told myself, but not now. Right now I was pregnant and with a three-year-old, and my job didn't pay enough to support us.

Chapter 20

Christmas was over and it was time to go back to work. I hated when holidays came around; it meant I would be home more. I loved my time at work, except that Nicole wasn't there. She loved her daycare and I could tell it was her peaceful time too. More and more, time away from home seemed like the only peace we got.

I left the house and headed to daycare. I could see it was going to be one of those mornings. Nicole didn't want to let go of me.

As soon as I pulled up to the daycare, the tears started falling. She had been extremely quiet for a few days, almost sad.

"Nicole, now you know Mommy has to go to work," I said as I lifted her out of the car.

Her tears started falling faster. She reached for my neck and it felt as if she was holding on for dear life. I pulled her away enough to look at her.

"Nicole, what's wrong, Honey? Why are you so sad?"

"Mommy, I don't want you to die."

"Well Baby, I'm not going anywhere that I know of. Why would you be worried about such a thing?"

"I heard Daddy tell you he wishes you would die!" she wailed.

I looked away, having lost my breath.

"Oh Sweetie, Daddy was joking. He sometimes says stuff that he thinks is funny, but no one else does," I laughed slightly. "I promise you I'm not dying. I'm not leaving you. You are stuck with me for a very long time, little girl!" I thought for a moment longer, "Nicole, did you get out of your bed last night, Sweetie?"

"Yes, I was thirsty and when I went to come get you, I heard Daddy talking really mean to you. He wasn't joking. Mommy, it was scaring me so I went back to my bed."

"I promise you, I pinky promise you, Mommy is not going to die. I am right here." I gave her neck raspberries and she giggled. "Remember, for this afternoon, think about a high-low for the day.

I could see yhat she was reassured I wasn't going to die and felt safe once again, so I walked her into the daycare."

"Nicole, don't say anything to others about what you heard last night, okay Baby. They won't think it's funny either."

"Okay Mommy! I love you, and Mommy, my low was this morning."

She was so smart. I watched her walk to the door, almost skipping, and tears burned the corner of my eyes. Once in my car, I could no longer be subdued. I drove far enough away so that no one would catch me crying.

The first face I saw when I entered work was Lisa's. She knew. I made my way to my office, her trailing not far behind.

"What happened this time, Eve?"

"I'm okay, Lisa,"

"No you are not. Tell me."

We had become such good friends, and I treasured her friendship. We had similar backgrounds, but she left her abuser and was free.

"I went to drop Nicole off this morning Lisa, and she was so sad." I told her what Nicole had said.

"Eve, I know you don't think you can, Honey, but it's time to leave. You cannot let your child see you like this, it isn't fair, and I'm not one to judge. Look how long it took me to leave."

"I know Lisa, I know but, but, oh my God, how did I get here?" I busted into tears, "I'm pregnant, I can't leave!"

I saw her face drop and it only confirmed how stuck I felt.

How will I ever leave now? How will I ever be able to provide a safe, secure home for two children? Lisa took my hands in hers and reassured me that it wasn't the end of the world.

"Eve, you can. I believe you will find the courage to leave, it may not be this week, but I know you will Eve. God will provide a way for you to take care of your babies. Trust Him."

I made my way through the rest of the day, dreading the conversation I had to have with Seth. I wondered what it must feel like to know you are pregnant and have the joy and excitement that went along with telling your spouse. How great that must be. I envied those women at that moment. I wondered if they even knew how blessed they were.

After picking Nicole up from daycare, I made the nervous drive home.

Home.

It has never felt like a home. He made sure I knew nothing there was mine. After going over it again and again in my mind, I decided I would tell Seth that night and get it over with. Either way, I knew it would be bad.

I made sure dinner was prepared. I believed I had everything the way it should be. I prayed. He finally decides to come home a little after eight. Not that I cared what time. Typically, the longer he stayed gone, the better for me and Nicole. But the longer it took that night, the more my anxiety increased. I fixed his plate and brought it to him, along with a cold beer. He had already had too many by the looks of it, but I was hoping maybe that beer would knock him out. I sat on the couch next to his chair. Time to rip off the Band-Aid off.

"Seth, I have something to tell you."

"What? What the hell is it?

I knew to just spit it out before I lost my nerve, "I'm pregnant." He didn't respond. The only evidence that he'd heard me was that his fork had stopped mid-air, half-way to his mouth.

"I'm about eight weeks along."

I saw the look on his face and I knew I wouldn't get a hug, a kiss, or even a smile. He jumped up and tossed his plate to the floor. He pulled me up by my arms and forced me to look him in the eye.

"You are a no-good whore."

Thankfully, Nicole was in her room watching Barney and could not hear him. He didn't even care anymore if she did.

"I'm not a whore. I have never been unfaithful to you and never will be."

"It's not my child, so when it's born we will have one of those DNA tests done. I be damned if I help raise another child that's not mine!"

I prayed Nicole didn't hear him; it would surely break her heart.

"Seth, Nicole is your child and this one will also be your child. I know you don't believe me, but it's true. You can take whatever test you need to. I'm telling the truth."

"Shut up, grab me another plate and get me another beer, too. While you're at it grab yourself one, sit down and have a drink with me.

"You know I don't drink, but even if I did, I wouldn't because I'm pregnant,"

"I don't care what you are. Maybe that's a way to get rid of the little bastard you're carrying; save yourself the embarrassment of being labeled a slut."

"I'm not drinking a beer Seth."

"Did you forget your place here, Honey?"

"No, I'm aware that I am nothing but a maid to you." He laughed. "I know my place; you make it very clear on a daily basis."

"Like I said, whore, get me another beer. I want to watch a movie. You may want to put Nicole to bed; what I'm watching I don't think you would want her to see."

I put Nicole in her bed and told her I was going to leave the movie on so she could watch it. Once she fell asleep, I'd go back in to turn it off. I made sure I turned it up a little more than it was, just to drown out any noises she might hear.

"I love you Nicole, sweet dreams. Oh I almost forgot, what was your high-low today."

"Well Mommy, my low was this morning when I thought you were going to die and my high was when you picked me up Mommy, and you didn't die."

Her high should be about a piece of candy someone gave her, and her low about a child that pulled her hair.

"Good night, Sweetheart."

I walked down the hall and I could hear Seth talking to someone. When I entered, Liz from down the street was in our living room. Why was she here? Immediately, the room became cold, I could feel the sinister thoughts in their heads.

"Hi Liz, how are you?"

"I'm good. Seth said I should come over, you two needed some company. Everything okay?" I could see she was honestly concerned.

"Sit down Eve, let's watch a movie."

I looked at Liz and she seemed excited.

"It's okay," she says to me. "Really, come here." Liz walked over to me and I felt her hand travel up my shirt.

"Stop! What...what are you doing?" I jumped back.

"Eve, sit down Darlin'. Liz ain't going nowhere. Liz and me have some unfinished business to attend to. Stay or go. Either way, Liz is staying."

I was confused for a second until Seth started the movie. Liz began what I'm assuming they had started. She had straddled Seth like a horse. I left the room as fast as I could.

I had to leave. I knew it then.

I fell asleep crying and woke to Liz lying next to me and Seth on the other side of her. Liz was asleep, but Seth was wide awake.

"Come on Baby, it's your turn. Don't be sad. I was just having some fun. I mean look at her.

You have to admit she's everything you're not. How could I turn her away. She's been coming on to me for months. I only gave her what she wanted. You women are all the same. Only, I love you Darlin'."

I rolled back over, hoping he would fall asleep, I knew better. I heard him walk to my side of the bed. Before long he was on top of me, holding me down. I couldn't move. I was frozen, and in that moment my decision was made.

After it was over and he went to sleep, I went into Nicole's room and crawled in bed with her. I brought my clothes for work with me, so I wouldn't have to go into that room again. When my alarm went off the next morning, I got Nicole and myself dressed and headed for the front door.

"Eve, thank you for last night. Can't wait to do it again."

"Mommy, why is Ms. Liz here? Did she spend the night with you?"

I didn't answer.

My mind was focused on dropping Nicole off at daycare and the drive to work where I would tell Lisa what hell he put me through the night before.

"Oh my God Eve, that's terrible! Honey, you

have to leave. You have to get a plan."

"I know I do, Lisa. My decision was made last night. Only, I have to wait until the baby is born. I promise you, once that is behind me I will leave."

Over the next few weeks Seth came home some nights, some he didn't. Many times I'd wished he wouldn't come home at all. I saw his truck at Liz's house, along with quite a few other cars a couple of times.

He'd come in and pass out.

Chapter 21

I went through the next few months in a daze. Six months along and the bump on my stomach became increasingly noticeable. It was hard keeping up with Nicole, and also making sure Seth had no reason to get angry. Not that he ever really needed a reason. He stayed gone a good bit and I was glad.

After a doctor's appointment, I decided not to go back to work and simply go home to take a nap. Nicole was at daycare and I knew I still had several hours.

I walked through the door and smelled perfume. I heard the moans coming from the bedroom before I actually figured out where the smell was coming from, in my mind.

I guess they heard the door and they become silent. Not long after, the door opened and Liz walked out in nothing, but her bra. "Seth, your maid is home."

I stood there rubbing my baby bump in complete disbelief.

Finally, I turned and left. I drove to daycare and picked up Nicole. She was so excited about going to Chuck E Cheese, that it took the edge off some. Seeing her smile always made what was wrong, seem a little less wrong.

I made a mental note to call my dad. He hadn't been feeling well.

Nicole had a blast. We laughed and had a really good time until out of nowhere, I got a sense of urgency that it was time for us to leave.

I started feeling very panicky. The traffic was horrible and I couldn't get home fast enough.

For some reason I felt that I needed to call my dad.

"Daddy?"

"Hello, Eve. How about you and Nicole take a ride up here this weekend? I would love to see my granddaughter."

"Dad, is there something you aren't telling me? I can tell there is something you aren't telling me."

"It can wait until the weekend Sweetheart. See you Saturday?"

I agreed and told him I loved him.

"And I love you too, Baby."

Seth was standing by the hallway staring at me. I saw Liz sneak out the back door so Nicole wouldn't see her again. I guess she had enough decency to at least do that. Nicole went to her room.

"Where's my dinner, Eve?" I fell back against the chair with the force behind his slap.

"What do you want for dinner, Seth?"

"Don't worry about it now, I'm going out."

I sat for a few moments, then went to find where Nicole was. Luckily, she was playing with her dolls, not a care in the world. In a few short months, I knew I would have another sweet little girl to protect from the truth. I prayed for the strength to make it through, until I could find a way to leave.

Seth didn't come home for a few days, which was a blessing to us. I woke up early Saturday morning ready to make the trip to see Dad. I got Nicole and myself dressed, and as I opened the door to leave, Seth was standing there.

"Where do you think you are going, Eve?"

"Nicole, go get in the car, Baby. Buckle your seatbelt how Mommy taught you okay?"

"Okay Mommy. Bye Daddy. I love you."

He either didn't hear her or didn't care. He didn't respond.

"Again, where do you think you are going?"

"To my father's, Seth. He invited us to go, so I'm going."

"I didn't say you could go"

"Why do you care where I go?"

"You are disgusting, Eve. I can barely stand the sight of you. I would venture to say your father will be very disappointed in you. Fat pig."

I moved away from him, in hopes he would let me leave. I walked to the car and when I shut the door and locked it, I breathed a sigh of relief.

I finished buckling up, and Nicole and I made the long drive to see my dad.

~ ~ ~

I arrived at Dad's and felt an even deeper relief. I knew he had been really sick recently and just couldn't shake it, but I knew now, Nicole and I were safe.

Truly.

My dad didn't want me to know. He was worried it would complicate my pregnancy, but he could no longer hide that he had stage IV lung cancer.

It hit me harder than any of Seth's punches. He let me know that he would be starting chemotherapy and radiation.

As the months passed, it wore his body down. I remember being two weeks overdue praying Ann would make her arrival before Monday. I knew come Monday Dad would be gone for two weeks, undergoing his chemo treatments in Jackson. I called him Saturday night against Seth's wishes, and he told me to drink a virgin bloody Mary and eat a pizza, "and Baby, it's a full moon tonight. Wish on the full moon," I did just as he said, not that I believed in superstition, but at that point I'd have tried just about anything.

I needed him to be there with me on that day, he just had to be.

It was midnight on the dot when my water broke. I ran around panicking trying to get everything I needed. Seth was not happy about waking up at midnight, but it couldn't be avoided. If I could have, I would have driven myself. We dropped Nicole off at Mrs. Carol's, I hated to call her so late, but she acted like she hadn't minded at all. We got to the hospital exactly an hour later. Seth had already found a chair in the lobby and was almost asleep, when the nurse called for him. I heard him say "Yes Darlin', anything for you." She looked at me as if to say, "*poor you.*"

She had no idea.

Labor became intense. Mom fed me ice chips, put a cool rag on my head, and rubbed my hand.

"Breathe, Baby. Just breathe," she kept repeating.

At some point, Seth disappeared from the room.

"Eve, honey, you know your dad would come in here if he could, but he can't. With the chemo treatments, his immune system is just too weak, but he will be waiting for you when it's over."

Dad.

The doctor instructed the nurse to get the father.

"No need to get the father," Mom stopped the nurse.

We hadn't seen Seth for about the entire time. It was a relief to be honest. I could no longer stand the sight of him; he repulsed me. For whatever reason, I was also hurt. Thankfully, I had my mom helping me and that was really all I needed.

Ann was born and we were settled in a

regular room on the nursery wing. Dad came in carrying Nicole, who had a fistful of M&M's in her hand and a big smile on her face. Dad always had M&M's and all of his grandchildren knew it. Thankfully, Mom had him pick Nicole up from Mrs. Carol's, because she knew Seth wouldn't have remembered. It had been a few weeks since I had seen my dad. It was heart wrenching to see how much he had deteriorated in that short amount of time.

"Dad, what are you-"

"Baby, it's okay. I'm okay." He leaned over and kissed me on the forehead.

I remember thinking he was so strong, never one to complain. Only I knew that didn't make someone strong. That was just his by-product. Maybe crying and complaining is strong to someone else, their by-product of standing up for themselves.

He never wanted anyone's pity; to him it was a sign of weakness, and there I was pitying him.

Dad placed Nicole on the side of my bed and leaned in to pick up Ann. I watched, making sure I caught every little baby noise he made to her. Every little smile. The way he put his finger under her little fingers. Ann wrapped her tiny hand around his finger. I watched as he counted all her toes and gently kissed her on the forehead, as he had always done Jean and me. I watched him stare at Ann and knew he was thinking he'd never see this child run into his arms or call him Pawpaw. That this child wouldn't even remember him. I saw the tears well up in his eyes; he handed Ann back to me and quickly excused himself.

When he returned, the smile was back. It was just a front, one meant to protect the ones he loved. Dad reached for my hand and thanked me for such a beautiful gift.

"She is just as beautiful as you were the day you were born. I have to go now, Eve. I can't stay in the hospital long for fear of illness. I love you. I will see you soon." He bent down, kissed Nicole on the forehead, and was gone.

Looking back, I know this was a gift from God. He knew how much I needed my dad to not only be there, but also to hold my child. It was the only time he ever saw Ann.

Seth finally made his way to the room. As usual, he sat in the corner not the least bit interested, waiting to escape again. Every nurse that came in, Seth made a sexual innuendo towards; I was so embarrassed with his disgusting display of disrespect and indecency. He was pathetic. I knew he did it on purpose to humiliate me.

Then again, looking back, it was all purposeful. The hardest thing to accept about abuse, is that. When you have excuses like "he didn't mean to" or "he was angry" or "drunk," then you rationalize how you've let such horrible things happens to you.

Truth is, actions are purposeful. You either take action to change for the better or take action to change for the worse.

Either way, behavior is actionable.

Chapter 22

Ann had only been home for a few days when Seth decided to invite friends over to celebrate her birth. I knew it was only an excuse to drink more. I was inside feeding Ann, he and his friends were outside. I could hear how belligerent he was already and it was early. I sat, knowing later would be bad. His friend Danny was standing behind me, looking at Ann when Seth walked in.

"Hey man, this sure is a fine little girl you got here, Seth. She is as pretty as her momma." I cringed as the words left his mouth. Later, after everyone left, I was in the kitchen cleaning up the mess left behind. Nicole was in her room playing and Ann was finally sound asleep in her bassinet.

"Eve, come here please," Seth said calmly from the door to his bedroom. It had become his, but looking back that's how it had always been. I was consumed with an overwhelming sense of dread, as I walk towards the door.

It is surprising what you can endure ,knowing it will soon come to an end.

I no sooner stepped into our room and I'm knocked to the floor. The hit was so hard I may have blacked out; if so it wasn't for long.

"How dare you sit there and let a man look down your shirt! I saw what you were doing. You think I'm an idiot?"

"What? I was feeding our child Seth." I raised my voice, "I wasn't flashing your friend!" I knew the tone of my voice set him off. I braced myself.

I saw movement out of the corner of my eye. Nicole she was standing at the door, looking at me. She slowly looked up at Seth.

"What are you doing, Daddy?"

"None of your business little girl, go to your room."

She, a four-year-old could sense what was taking place.

"Go back to bed, Sweetie," I whispered.

165

She slowly walked toward me and sat in my lap. "It's okay." I ran my hand softly over her hair and said, "Sweetie, go back to bed and I will come tuck you in."

She leaned back into me and rested her head on my chest. Seth uncurled his fist and let his arm fall by his side. Nicole saved me.

I was being saved by my child, the one I'm supposed to protect. She had become my protector. With an immense amount of guilt and relief, I let her.

He walked to the living room, sat in his chair and fell asleep.

I held Nicole and thought back to the days when I was younger. When church was something my mom built our lives around. The congregation was our extended family. We were there pretty much every time the doors were open. We enjoyed potluck dinners and played in the church yard while the adults prepared the meals and talked amongst themselves.

It was such a safe place. I thought of Kevin, another safe place. I think of the woman I would've been with him, accepted, loved and protected.

I knew something had to change. I had to take action to change for the better, or take action by deciding to do nothing and change for the worse. I just needed to find the strength to do it.

It seemed the moment I fell asleep, Seth was behind me. He did what he always did and took what he wanted, without regard to my having just had a baby. The next morning I was bleeding heavily and I knew something was wrong. I dressed Nicole and Ann quickly and headed to the hospital.

"Okay, when did you give birth, Honey?" the nurse asked.

"Three weeks ago." I saw the alarm in her eyes.

"You know you aren't supposed to..."

"Yes Ma'am, I know," I hung my head.

Nicole got out of the chair next to the bed and walked over to me. She placed her small hand on my arm, "It's okay, Mommy. Daddy's not here."

I immediately started crying. I tried not to, but it was unstoppable.

"Thank you, Sweetie." I patted her arm with my free hand. I looked back up of the nurse, "Please don't ask questions, just help me."

"Sure Honey, we will get the bleeding under control and take good care of you."

She didn't ask anymore questions. She was so kind and treated me with respect.

"You know God can take care of you, right?"

I nodded slightly.

"You gotta let Him. Think of Him as a gentleman opening a door for you. You can walk in, or walk away."

I heard her tell someone in the ER that she wasn't supposed to be on duty today, but her shift had been extended. She said she believed she was there for a reason.

I believed she was also. I've never forgotten her. She could've made me feel small and stupid, but instead she reminded me whose child I was.

~ ~ ~

My father's health steadily declined and the weekend trips just weren't enough for me, but it was the best I could do. It was hard to find someone to watch the girls every weekend. I wished they could've come with me, but it wasn't safe for Dad.

Seth had no family; I think an uncle or two, but no siblings or parents. He was raised by his grandfather, who had long since passed away. My kids never met one single member of his family. He was a loner most of his life. The story I got from one of his friends was, he left home at sixteen and never looked back. His parents were drug addicts, so it wasn't a surprise he would follow suit. Although alcohol was his biggest poison.

I was offered time off from work, with pay, to be with my father. I couldn't believe they would offer such a generous sentiment; most places were all about the bottom line. However, I couldn't take them up on their generosity. I had children that couldn't be around my father due to his illness, and I knew I had no one to help for that long. To this day, I regret not finding a way to make it work.

The call. It wouldn't be long now. Mom suggested we make funeral arrangements in advance. She said that once Dad passed, it would be much harder to do.

I don't remember crying that day. I remember going through all the emotions, but actually crying wasn't a result. I was more concerned for Jean, Warren, and Clark. I wanted them to be okay. I wished in that moment I could have taken all of their hurt and shielded them from the pain, but I was barely able to withstand my own in that moment.

We opened the Toolbox and on the top divider found a group of envelopes, one addressed to us all, and then additional ones addressed to each of us individually. We agreed to wait until after planning the funeral, to read them.

Funeral homes were always cold to me. I remembered shaking as I sat next to my mom, aunt, stepmother, and siblings making funeral arrangements. I wrote out my father's obituary. My mind was in such a fog, that I don't know how I made it through the entire process.

When it was time to pick out my father's coffin, I turned to look back at Jean, Warren, and Clark. They looked so small, so helpless.

We made our way up the stairs and entered the room. Everywhere I looked there was death. Coffins, big ones, small ones, pretty ones, not so pretty ones, were all stacked over one another.

I was only twenty-eight years old. I didn't want to be there. I didn't want to lose my dad. I told everyone that I needed to step outside for a moment. I just needed a bit of fresh air.

I wasn't outside long, when I heard someone approaching.

Mom.

She sat beside me on the front steps of the funeral home.

"Eve, you know your father was a simple man. He wouldn't want anything extravagant or fancy. I know I'm no longer married to your father, but I still know him well. Whatever you kids decide, will be just fine. Keep in mind, your father will be with God. No more pain. He'll probably be up there telling God how to hunt and fish. He'll likely be doing that himself, waiting for all of us. He will finally be at peace." she leaned over and kissed my forehead. "You all can do this, Eve. You have each other. You have me. And if you find that you simply can't do it, no one will be upset with you, Sweetie. I have confidence you will find the strength you need to handle anything."

I made my way back up the dreaded stairs into the room filled with caskets. I was still somewhat in a daze; but a little clearer. I could still see the color of the linen, blue, a beautiful shade of blue, on one of the caskets on the bottom row across the room. I walked over to it and looked down at the beautiful light blue fabric. I spotted a flash of color. Something small within the folds of the casket. I leaned in and moved the material to get a better look. Of all things, it was an M&M. It was right there in the creases of the linen.

My first thought was, how did it get here?

It didn't matter how, to me it was a kiss from Heaven. A comfort.

Dad and his M&M's. I thought back to all the times he brought us M&M's. It was the only candy he brought for the grandkids and ninety-nine percent of the time, it was he who ate most of the pack that was meant for them. I asked everyone what they thought, but I had already made my choice. That casket was perfect, and they agreed.

I never did question where that M&M may have come from. Probably from a child who tailed along with someone who was tasked to make that same decision for someone they loved. I only knew that it made what I had to do that day, in that moment, a lot easier. I'd like to believe it was a precious gift. Like God had that child, on that day, drop that M&M, for me. I closed my eyes and imagined the child looking around on the floor. Bending down, looking under the casket; turning from side to side in hopes of finding it. I also imagined God allowing that M&M to stay in the folds of that coffin, just for my peace. I'd heard of other people having those kinds of moments, ones where they thought in such intricate detail how God provided for them in their need, but really thought they mostly seemed farfetched.

Then this happened, and I understood. When you are in a crisis, you look everywhere for that one sign that makes it all better.

You usually find it.

The funeral was planned, and I didn't know how many more days were left to prepare my heart for that.

Impossible.

Chapter 23

That evening after agreeing on the funeral plans, Jean, Clark, Warren and I sat down in the living room at Aunt Nan's house, staring at the toolbox.

It seemed like an eternity before I was able to reach and touch it. I put my hand onto the cool metal and slowly lifted the top and then the tray. The first item was a folded napkin. It was odd, like a disposable one that you get in your McDonald's bag. I thought maybe he cried on it and that made it special.

Maybe it was just a napkin. I set it aside and pulled another item off the top. Dad's watch.

"Wait," Clark said, "I don't think I'm ready."

"None of us are ready. I don't think we'll ever be."

Clark shook his head in agreement and I continued.

The watch was one we had given him for Father's day, when we were just kids. Mom obviously picked it out. We knew how special it was to him. Even when it was running slow at one point, he still wore it until he got it repaired.

I kissed it lightly and placed it aside with the napkin. In doing so, it caused a part of the napkin to lift a bit and I saw writing inside.

Opening it gently, I read the words. Part of my childhood came flooding back like a river. I was transported back to sitting on the porch, Nana with her old coffee mug, me in my pajamas. I listened intently as she told me the story.

"I told them, it was a lovebug. Your dad and your Uncle Rob laughed at me, but it was. Oh, Rob said lovebug season was still months away, but I knew it was a sign from God. There was no other explanation."

"Why would a lovebug be a sign from God?" I had asked, having never heard the story before.

"Because, I was telling your dad that God works in mysterious ways. For example," she looked at me, lifted her brows and said, "lovebugs. There seems to be no purpose for them, but God made them. So they must have some purpose. I was explaining, that even if we don't always know what God's plan is, we can trust He knows and that everything will be okay. I told your dad he would get better, when he was so sick as a child. To be honest, I didn't know. I must admit, I was afraid he wouldn't make it through. I was so grief stricken."

"And dad felt better because of lovebugs?" I was definitely more confused than before she started explaining.

"No, Honey. It wasn't about your dad. This story is about me. I'd had a true lack of faith; missteps that people don't talk about, but should, because we all have them. I didn't trust God that everything would be alright, even if your dad passed. You know, none of us is promised another day."

"And... a lovebug helped you learn this?" I thought for sure Nana's mind was starting a quick mental decline.

"Let me finish, Dear. I had just reassured your dad that God had a plan. He cares for us and concerns Himself with the things that concern us. Like lovebugs, we don't always see the plan, but it's still there. I walked out of the hospital to cry for a few minutes. Again, I was having a crisis with my own trust in God, when just then a lovebug, months before the season was to even begin, floated slowly through the air in front of my face. I watched as it made a slow descent and landed right on top of the Mother's ring the kids had gotten me for Christmas two years before, right on top of the stone that represented your dad's birth month. I felt immediate peace. I knew that lovebug, in the dead middle of winter, was a sign from God on this earth that He was there."

"Okay, Nana." She was definitely losing it. Every time I saw a lovebug through the years, I thought of how crazy old Nana saw it as a sign.

I looked back down at the napkin and read it again:

God works in mysterious ways, you just have to be looking to see it.
My sign from God: one single lovebug.

I guess mine was an M&M. That small round piece of candy didn't make me feel nearly the way Nana had always said that little lovebug made her feel, but it was something.

Jean lifted the next object out, Nana's old coffee mug. We all laughed.

"Man, all these years Dad drank his coffee

out of that old thing," Warren commented.

"Do you remember when you almost broke it?" I asked Jean.

"Yes. I don't think Dad was ever as mad at me as he was that day," Jean replied.

"Yeah, he never left the cup on the end table again," we all laughed.

"And we never ran in the house again," Jean added and we all laughed again.

Clark had sifted through a few of the items without taking any of them out.

"I don't get it, it's all kinda junk," he said.

"Yeah," Warren said, "I think he just meant to leave us the letters, and he put them in there and left it in the middle of the floor so we'd find them."

"I agree," Jean said as she replaced the items we had taken out. "Let's read."

"I don't know, I kind of want the mug...and maybe the watch," I said.

"Have at it," Jean replied and the boys agreed in unison.

I picked up the envelopes and gave each of them, the one with their name on it. They all simply held theirs, not really knowing what to do. I sat my envelope in my lap and opened the one addressed to us all.

Eve, Jean, Warren & Clark
You each have brought me so much joy
through the years. In this life, I have
had some really low points. I wish
doctors would've found the problem
much earlier, so I could've understood
my mood swings better. But the latter
part of my life was well lived and I
am thankful to God for it.
I have enclosed a letter to each of
you. To be clear I'll say a few things
here so nobody fusses, which I hope
you guys wouldn't do anyway, but death
makes people do weird things.
The land goes to each of you. I
already have the breakdown of lots
drawn so you can each get the piece
I think best suits you. It's obvious,
but again I'm stating it here so
there is no room for fussing.
Eve, you get The Campground. I had
hoped you'd one day repair and move
into Nana's house, but you don't have
to. Lord knows I couldn't set foot
in it. If it stays simply a place for
you to escape to, then I hope it will
serve you well and often.
Jean, The Clearing is yours, for when
you need a break, a nap away from all
my precious grandbabies. It's there
for you. I also hope all your kids will

enjoy it for years to come. Take a break often and don't feel guilty about it.

Warren, The Woods. It always was home to you, the trees and the solitude. Let it stay that way. I hope one day you marry and raise a family there, but if you don't and it stays a weekend retreat, I'll be just as happy.

Clark, The Fishing Hole. I know you always talked about putting a house right there in front of the pond and I have always loved that idea. Two bits of advice, don't build too close or the mosquitos will bother you something awful, and don't stop the townspeople from fishing there. That pond fed many a family when nobody else would. You four stay close. I can't tell you what to do with your lives, but my individual letter just about sums up my thoughts for each of you. I didn't have much other than the land, but I want my hunting stuff, guns and all, and the old Ford to go to Warren, I know it will all be put to good use at "The woods." The fishing stuff, including the boat and trailer, to Clark, so he can enjoy his favorite pastimes anytime he wants at The Fishing Hole. The tractor and all the

attachments, to Jean. It'll help keep
The Clearing looking good for a nap.
The toolbox to Eve, as sentimental as
she is these small things will help her
decide about the house.
I love you all so much. You have made
life worth living.
Dad

We all cried and hugged. All four of us loaded up in the Ford. Warren put the toolbox in the bed and we went to the hospital. Dad wasn't awake of course, but we sat in his room and told old stories. We laughed and cried, then laughed some more. When the nurse came in and suggested we come back the next day, we knew it was time to leave. Clark wanted to stay another night and we knew it was important to him, so we agreed.

As soon as we arrived back at Aunt Nan's, I asked Warren if he'd bring the toolbox to the back porch for me. It was then, in the quiet of the night as everyone in the house made their way to bed, that I opened my letter. I know I wasn't supposed to until after he had passed, but I just couldn't wait any longer.

Eve,
Don't rush through this. By now, I am gone and so my wish for you is that you go somewhere alone and go through the list as I have written it. Don't skip ahead or rush through the things in the toolbox. First thing, get the mug and go get a cup of coffee in it, then continue. Eve, I know you didn't wait until I was gone, you have always been my impatient child who doesn't like surprises.
It's okay.

I slowly opened the top and reached for Dad's mug, Nana's mug. I went into the kitchen and perked a pot of coffee, then returned to the back porch with the cup gripped firmly in my hand, afraid I would drop it. It was nostalgic. Of course I wanted to rush through each thing, but the letter said not to. It was important to Dad.

The coffee steamed through the air and a rush of memories assailed me.

Dad was attached to that cup so much so, that even when company came over, he would put it to the side so no one else would use it. It was his mom's so I get that now, but as a teenager it was just weird.

Who cares that much for a coffee cup? Only, now, I understand. I could see myself pushing it to the back of the cabinets or moving it to the side so no one else would get it before me, because, truly it was more than a coffee cup, it was a legacy.

I know it sounded silly, but it's not when you are holding it, remembering so many moments it was a part of. A witness to.

I picked up the letter and read on and Dad's words lifted off the page:

If you have a cup of coffee in that mug, you can continue with #1

1.   Nana's Coffee Mug
My first memory with the mug was getting a spanking. I knew when I picked it up, that if I were caught, I'd get one, so it was well deserved. I couldn't claim I didn't know better, 'cause everyone knew: Do not touch Ma's coffee mug. But for some reason it made it that much more valuable. It was like a shiny new toy car that you just had to touch because it shined so good. Needless to tell you this, because you've heard that story probably one too many times, I never

touched that mug again, until after she passed. Then, I knew I would never let it go. Remember where you came from. Remember the good stuff and hold tight.
Just don't forget the spankings, so you know when to let go.

I knew he was telling me, that at some point I'd have to move forward and let go of him, but I also knew that was impossible. He really knew it, too. Still, I was so thankful for that coffee mug. I leaned back into a rocking chair and inhaled the scent of the freshly ground coffee, then took a sip. I also knew I'd have to leave the cup at Aunt Nan's, because Seth would surely break it. There was no limit to how far he would go to hurt me.

I bent forward and lifted the letter to continue with the list. Number two.

You'll need number two and three together.

2.   Flashlight
You have always been so afraid. Afraid of everything, even your own shadow. I thought I could help you find confidence and maybe

things wouldn't seem so threatening,
but you just always felt like you
needed someone to protect you.
What you didn't see about yourself,
that everyone around you does see,
is that Eve, you are the protector.
You find the wounded and try to
heal them. You find the fight and
try to soothe it. You find the lost,
and try to save them. Unfortunately,
that leaves you in the dark. You leave
yourself behind while you try to fix
everything and everyone else. One
of my favorite memories of us is
around that campfire, laughing and
talking and making S'mores while
everyone else was running around
playing. In that moment you weren't
afraid, you weren't rescuing anyone,
and you weren't sacrificing yourself
for others. I'm glad I didn't bring a
flashlight that night, if I had, you
and I would never have ended up in
front of that fire just being us. It's
important to watch your way, it's also
important to sometimes just lose your
way and find yourself. The dark will
give way to the light Eve.
You can't always rescue everyone.

Immediately, tears fell and rolled down my cheeks, I could taste the salty mix of mascara and foundation from each tear that fell. I could barely see enough to lift Dad's old worn flashlight out of the box. The one he always freaked out about when someone didn't put it back where it belonged. I laughed unintentionally. I reread the last few sentences, as I tried to flick on the flashlight, with no luck. I went inside and looked through Aunt Nan's pantry to find batteries. I didn't expect the flashlight to work, but I'd hoped. After I loaded the batteries, I took a deep breath and flicked the switch. And the flashlight came to life. I wanted to stop for a moment and just catch my breath, but Dad had said that number three went with number two so I read on:

3. Softball

I've always said it is okay to be scared, but you can't let that fear paralyze you to the point of not living. Sometimes our minds are our worst enemy. Mine definitely was. I have problems doctors are just now starting to really understand. I don't think it'll ever be understood fully, because who can really understand the mind. However, Eve, I want you to try to understand yourself and your boundaries. You can push yourself to have a fuller life in spite of the random thoughts and bouts of depression. Don't sacrifice your own happiness for someone else, because one, you'll never understand them, and two, you'll never fully understand yourself if you are always trying to focus on the minds of others. Push yourself past your limits to achieve your goals. Just as pitching this softball into my shop door, now your shop door, with that small strike zone was impossible, it became possible the more you focused and practiced. Sometimes I think that's our minds: focus on what good you've got and practice with what's left.

I lifted my old shabby and frayed softball out of the metal box and held it as though I was about to pitch the best I'd ever thrown. Then I stood and used that flashlight to go out into the yard and pitch that softball for hours into the large field behind Aunt Nan's, thinking on what my dad had said.

Chapter 24

Ihad put the toolbox out of my mind on purpose, too much to think about that morning. I closed it the night before, after crying and pitching for hours, and placed it back into the room where I was staying.

I woke early and had just started breakfast, when Clark walked in the front door. He said Dad had a bad night; it would be soon, he felt. Eventually the smell of breakfast brought everyone else down to the table. We didn't talk much, but we all recognized the importance of being together, I think. Aunt Nan, Marie and her family were the only family we had left.

"When is Marie coming with the kids?" Clark

asked, just after he placed his fork on his plate.

Aunt Nan looked above his head to the clock on the wall, "Oh anytime now. Rich won't be coming until, well, you know, but she is bringing the kids and staying the weekend. It'll be nice to see her."

"I thought she always wanted to build a house next door here," Clark mentioned.

"Yes, she does, but Rich doesn't want to commute two hours to work, and until he's ready to start his own practice here, it just isn't feasible."

"We could help them get started though, on the house I mean," Warren said. "Weekends aren't much to offer, but it'd be a start."

"I'm game," Clark added, "We come up here anyway."

Aunt Nan's face lit up and I was sad to think I hadn't really noticed how worn down she had been looking.

"I think that is a great idea," she said. "I mean we need a lawyer here now. Mr. Puckett's been gone for nearly five years now and it's hard to find someone you can trust. Maybe a house would make it easier for Rich to make the move."

The boys agreed to talk it over with Rich when he came.

We spent the better part of the day at the hospital. Again, telling stories and hoping somehow Dad could hear. One of the nurses said she believed the patients could hear, but no one ever really knew for sure.

Mom showed up at the hospital around four, and we all went to eat with her in the hospital cafeteria. She asked if she could stay the night with Dad, instead of one of us. We knew it was like that day on the porch. This was her last goodbye.

When we made it back to Aunt Nan's, Marie and the kids were there. Supper was already on the table. I wasn't hungry since we'd just eaten, so I stayed at the table and visited a while. Marie was tired and the boys told her to go to bed and rest, they'd handle the kids. Once Marie had gone to bed, Warren and Clark went outside to play with the kids. I started cleaning the dishes with Aunt Nan.

"You know, I really hope Rich likes the idea of starting on a house," she said as she wiped away the water droplets from a plate and placed it on the shelf.

"Me too," I readily agreed.

"I also hope one day life leads you back here. I hope you will one day call this place home. While you sit on that porch and watch your grandkids roam the same paths you did as a child." she turned to look at me.

We finished the dishes and I went to my room. Immediately, I picked up the letter where I'd left it the night before and continued:

4. Handkerchief

I know how much you hated my handkerchief. You thought it always looked so dirty. I understood. Ma said she'd passed me her hanky one too many times to ever call it hers again. She taught me the importance of having one in my pocket.

I know it's got stains on it and I also know I could've bleached it clean many times throughout my life. But why would I want to remove the reminders of me being sick and throwing up blood? As much as you hated this old hanky, after washing and washing it, I realized I didn't mind so much if my blood stain on the top right was there forever. The bottom middle stain was from an oil leak I had in the old truck. When I came out from under that truck and you and Jean started giggling because I had a dot of oil on my forehead like I'd just come from mass on Ash Wednesday. I just couldn't bleach that out either. Top left: when your mom slit her finger open with that damn new filet knife I bought her for Mother's day. Faded in the background is a lot of sweat and tears. Bottom right, the blood from your lip when Ms. Faith called me to come rescue you from Seth.

All of those stains mean something, but most importantly they mean we all have blemishes on our lives, even the bad ones shouldn't be forgotten. Carry those with you so you can always remember where you've been and how far God's brought you.

I lifted the handkerchief, which had been tucked along one side of the toolbox and looked at it. All the stains he mentioned were there, faint, but there. I was set to continue, but also felt eager to stop. My life was a mess and there seemed to be no way out of it. Dad's words on paper made them more powerful somehow.

I looked at the next item and reached for it:

5. Deck of Cards

Fifty-two card pick up. Man you and Jean sure loved that game. When I sent those cards flying through the air, you both would giggle and chase those cards all over the place. It never got old to me, watching you girls giggling.

I know sometimes you feel like your life is like that deck of cards flying through the air. You feel like you are constantly picking up all those pieces, never knowing where they are going to land, and when the next set of cards will go flying. But one day Baby Girl, you are gonna find a new game, one where you control most of the cards, sure they'll always be the flyaways, but you'll find a steady balance.

Don't be afraid of that change.

"Get up, we've got to get to the hospital." Jean's voice shoved its way through the door and ripped me from sleep. I had fallen asleep at some point, holding Dad's letter.

"I'm up. I'm up," I said groggily. That day had been the worst so far. He had what people were referring to as the 'death rattle." It was something I'd never forget.

We stayed again until nighttime. It was my night, but Jean asked if she could stay instead. She felt it would happen that night, and she needed to be there with him.

I knew she needed that too.

Mom took on the task of driving back to Louisiana to pick up Nicole and Ann from Mrs. Carol's, who was gracious enough to take care of them while I was away. Seth said he was going to follow her in, but didn't want the hassle of the kids in the truck.

I sat on the floor staring at the toolbox. It was time to finish. I started reading:

6.   Dice

I know your mother would absolutely hate this, but get the dice out of the toolbox and hold them in your hand. I'm not asking you to gamble, I think you've done enough of that. Taking a gamble means you are trying something risky. It could have a great reward, but like most gambling, the odds are against you.

They are impossible to beat if you gamble with a cheater.

When you roll the dice Eve, it's important to know who you are playing with. Some opponents won't let you *win, even if you technically do, you won't leave that table alive.*

We all roll the dice when we decide to love someone, because love is a crapshoot. Often times, the odds are against us and a relationship won't work out. But when the right one comes along Eve, make sure you recognize and don't let the pains of your last roll prevent you from taking that chance again.

Seth didn't belong there; he offered no comfort. Most of what I'd known with him was pain and fear. I knew I had hit the losing odds; I just didn't have enough money to leave the table.

Chapter 25

The next day felt like life slowed down and everything was standing perfectly still.

Mom showed up that morning and it was so good to have the girls with me. Clark, of course, immediately took them fishing. Seth didn't follow Mom there like he said he was going to.

I can't say I wasn't relieved. That afternoon, the moment Seth entered Aunt Nan's front door, I felt a huge loss. I hated that he was there.. Not even two minutes later, the phone rang. It was Jean letting us know that Dad had passed.

I sat in place and stared off into nothing. I felt a firm hold on one of my arms, tugging at me.

"Get up," he harshly whispered. I could hear the bottle of liquor sloshing around in the duffle bag he had thrown over his shoulder. "You making a fool of yourself." Seth had made so many moments in my life about him. The sad thing was, I allowed it. He'd stolen so many moments, ones I could never get back. With my mind made up, I knew once I left he would never steal another moment from me again. He tugged harder and I stood. He followed me upstairs. I entered the room and he rushed in after me.

"I'm tired, I'm gonna take a nap. It was a long drive and I got lost." He stumbled over the toolbox and cursed, "Why the hell you got that old rusty thing in the middle of the damn room," he yelled. Soon, he climbed into bed and passed out.

I went downstairs and walked through the trails that led to The Fishing Hole. There I watched for hours as the girls and Clark laughed, fished, and of course threw the fish back, because I knew my girls wouldn't let Uncle Clark keep them. Ann was mostly babbling, too young to really fish.

I finally went back to the room and sat in front of that toolbox, listening to Seth snoring. I knew change wasn't coming anytime soon for

197

him. I began to read:

7. My watch
This thing really did take a licking
through the years. I don't know
if you were even old enough to
remember your momma giving me
this for father's day from you kids,
but it's been a treasure to me ever
since that day. It has traveled with
me through every moment of my life.
Good and the bad.
The day Ma passed. So hard I thought
I'd die too. It's okay to be that sad
sometimes, especially when you mourn
for those you love. People use excuses
of why they shouldn't cry, but God
gave you those tears, use 'em when
you need. Don't time your pain or
mourning, because it is, until it isn't.
I remember one day I had stopped
crying and knew the time had come
to move forward from that sadness
and start celebrating the life she had
led. This watch witnessed that day.
The day your momma asked me to
leave. I knew it was for the best.
Neither of us knew anything about
what caused me to have such highs
and lows back then. It must've been
exhausting for her and I commend

her for the years she dealt with it because she truly loved me. I know she did and to the day I die I still will love her. It's okay to love and still move on. On that day, when I looked down at this watch, I knew it was time to go.

The day I found out I had cancer (I ain't gonna capitalize it just 'cause) as I'd sat in my car after leaving the doctor's office, hours ticked by on this watch as I stared out the window in disbelief. Again, time was brought to the forefront.

This watch was also there when you had my sweet granbabies, when Jean got married, when the boys graduated. This watch went fishing and hunting with me.

A watch sees all, times everything, helps us be on time and know when we're late. Most important it helps us know when it's time to leave.

Keep watch on that time. Don't let it sneak up on you to find yourself looking back years later, wondering why you didn't just pay attention to what time it was.

That next morning I made sure to wake

early. Nicole and Ann slept with Aunt Nan and I was thankful as I lugged that toolbox down the stairs. I placed it on the floor in front of the fireplace and opened the letter.

That afternoon was Dad's funeral. I had prepared what I was going to say. Over and over again I read it, but it was missing something. After reading the last bit of the letter, I knew what I wanted to say.

Person after person shared memories of my father; some I knew, some I didn't. They all knew us though, he made sure everyone he met knew his children even if indirectly.

It was my turn. I stood, even after Seth had pinched me to sit still, and I walked to the platform. I leaned in a bit closer to the microphone.

"I had planned several things I wanted to say, but instead I thought I'd simply read some of Dad's own words. He wrote:

My life seemed sad because, well I got cancer (again no cap) but that ending doesn't define me. My weaknesses don't define me. My mental health doesn't define me. I wrote my own story, the one where I got to spend the best years of my life having you youngsters. Watching you grow. Learning to walk and talk. Hearing Jean say her abc's over and over because she was so proud of herself. Clark holding his first catch, then feeding us nearly every day until none of us could stand another bite of fish. Warren hauling his first buck home in the bed of that old Ford he'd fixed all by himself. You plugging that baseball through that target after nearly giving up a hundred times. I'll never regret my life, no matter how many mistakes I made.

It was nice that my father was loved. It was time for the last goodbye before they closed the casket.

The hardest part.

It would be the last time I would see his face in the physical sense. The last time he would be in the same room as me. The last time I'd be able to touch the hands that held us all as babies, played ball with us as kids, taught us how to fish, hunt, and love. The ones that held our hands many times throughout our lives. I stood there, looking down at Dad, next to my brothers and sister and felt not alone. We locked hands and said our goodbyes and didn't let go of each other's hands until we reached the parking lot. We stood for some time holding each other, before watching the coffin being loaded into the hearse.

We made the short drive to the grave site. The one song that played, still brings me to tears. My father requested it be played when that time came. It was beautiful and so very fitting.

"I know you are resting now, Daddy," I whispered. "See you soon."

Go rest high on that mountain by Vince Gill played. And I truly absorbed that song. It became forever etched on my heart. I knew I'd never be able to listen to it again without crying.

As I prepared to leave, I saw the headstone off in the distance that had always haunted me when I was younger, the little girl in the wheelchair. I hadn't thought about Kevin for a while. Twelve years later, I'm standing in the cemetery I hoped to never visit again, saying goodbye to someone else I love. The graveside service had been short; everything was the way Dad wanted.

I could see Seth out of the corner of my eye getting impatient, glaring at me. I had not really paid much mind to him all day. His narrative didn't matter anymore. His attendance was no longer relevant. I felt a heavy presence of peace wash over my body and soul, and I knew I had finally stepped into the darkness with a flashlight. And I knew in that moment, my father's words of wisdom had forever changed the direction of my life.

The girls were with Aunt Nan and Mom, safe. I told Seth I'd be back in a few minutes and even though he strenuously objected, I made the walk across the property to the pretty tree that watched over sweet Kevin's gravesite. The dirt had long since been covered in lush grass. There were those small wildflowers sprouting up around his headstone, that look like little daisies. I smiled, of course.

"Goodbye," it felt more definitive than it ever had before. "I have a lot to do. My life is about to change, and I get the feeling it is going to take every bit of strength I have ever had to get through it. Strength I'm not sure I have, but God does."

Time for me to go.

I gently pinched off a few of the tiny daisy-looking flowers and put them in my hair. I'm not sure why, it just felt like coming home. In the middle of that place, because it was where ones I love rested. Not just that cemetery, but that town also.

I turned to walk away and ever so softly, on that hot humid day in southern Mississippi, a gentle, warm breeze brushed the side of my cheek and flowed freely through my hair.

And a lovebug slowly landed on the tip of my nose.

~ ~ ~

Only two items remained in the toolbox that morning: A small notebook and a pen. The old worn notebook had a frayed piece of rope tied around it like it was a gift. I opened the last envelope, number eight.

8. Pen

Lastly, and I'm sure you are wondering why this cheap pen was left for last. Maybe you already guessed it. This pen is what I wrote the letters to you all with, also I left the journal of my last few months of life. Not much to learn there, but still I want you to read it, then pass it to the others. When I decided to write that journal, I did it in hopes that I could shed a new light on life. There's never been a time in my life when I wasn't

fighting against myself, to live
inside my own head. My soul always
knew the random thoughts weren't
true, but my mind just wouldn't
listen. I hid it pretty well, or so
I thought. Then, well I got cancer,
but that ending doesn't define me.
My weaknesses don't define me. My
mental health doesn't define me. I
wrote my own story, the one you
four need to hear. The one where I
got to spend the best years of my
life having you youngsters. Watching
you grow. Learning to walk and eat.
Hearing Jean say her abc's over and
over because she was so proud of
herself. Clark holding his first catch,
then feeding us nearly every day until
none of us could stand another bite
of fish. Warren hauling his first buck
home in the bed of that old Ford
he'd fixed all by himself. You plugging
that baseball through that target
after nearly giving up a hundred
times. I'll never regret my life, no
matter how many mistakes I made. I'll
focus on what it was to live and love.
You can write your own story, Eve, not
about your weaknesses or mistakes.
The new one, about your triumphs
and kids. About starting over. About

letting go. And mostly, about finding your way home.
It's easier than you think Eve, just pick up the pen.

THE END

Note from the Author

We all wonder what our lives would be like had we not met a certain person, or persons. I live with no regrets. Some people are in our lives for just a season, looking back I had a few of those seasons. However, I'm thankful the seasons change as they do. I know now that I am just where I was always meant to be. While at times the road that led me here became long and torturous, I have learned to take lessons and grow from all the bad. To use it to help others. I would not be here today, in this moment, with my best friend, my husband, if I had not experienced each season with the mindset it too will change. This season will also. One day, either he or I will be without one another as the seasons of our lives evolve.

So I am determined to enjoy this season to its fullest until then.

The social shunning.

Why is it that women still carry the majority of shame? Adultery? Such as Monica Lewinsky. She was single, yet it was her moral character that took the worst hit. Also, while rape and sexual assault victims are finally getting the sympathies they deserve, they still face the questions of their own responsibility. Even if publicly, society as a whole seem to support the victim, it is always the woman who gets the blame somehow.

Love, Yvette

Acknowledgements

There are so many people that made this book a possibility. First and foremost, I want to thank God for paving the way and guiding my every step. Without Your Grace, I would surely have fallen. With the uncertainty in our world today, I know the one truth is You. I remind myself in times of turmoil to simply "be still."

To my loving husband, Shannon Lee Whittington. Without you I would not have had the courage to finish what was started many years ago. You are my rock. You believed in me when I didn't believe in myself. I am so very blessed to have you as my husband. I love you to the moon and back and back again. Thank you for all that you do for me and for our family.

ACKNOWLEDGEMENTS

To my mother, Sherry. Thank you for being my biggest cheerleader, for pushing me to chase my dreams, and for believing that I could attain them. I, without a doubt, would not be the woman I am today without your guidance. You are, and always will be the smartest woman I have ever known. Your ability to write most certainly played a role in my passion for writing. I love you Mom. And to my bonus dad, Al. You are such a wonderful man; you embraced my mother and all of us with such ease. You inspire me with your kindness and gentle nature. I love you both.

To my father, although I lost you many years ago, I can still hear your words of wisdom and words of encouragement in all that I do. I am a carbon copy of you, our private nature, yet our ability to step out of that introverted state long enough to show others how much we care, is an attribute we share. You are always with me, in all that I do. I close my eyes and can see your face and I am assured, because of my faith, that I will one day be reunited with you, never to be apart again. I love you Daddy.

To my daughters, Breanna and Shelby. I have been blessed to be your mother. You two will always be all that is good in me. I wish I had slowed down more when you two were younger, long enough to cherish all those special moments. If I could give you each only one piece of advice, it would be to enjoy every moment, never let a moment pass having wished you would have said or done something only to realize it was too late.

To my siblings, Brandy and Will. You will always be my best friends. I can't imagine a life without either of you in it. Dad would be so proud of the adults we have become; the parents, grandparents and friends. So much of me is a part of you both. I love you both so very much.

Of course the editors who helped me clean up the manuscript and had endless patience. Deborah Dawn Hall, Alexis Jester, and Mallory at Tell It All, you three are incredible!

A very special thanks to Michelle Jester as my publisher, but above that, you are my dearest friend. Without your patience in guiding me to obtain my dream, I would surely have failed. I can never thank you enough for all that you have done to encourage me through this entire process.

Now, as my best friends, Michelle Jester and Wendy Logan: We laugh together, cry together and celebrate our victories, which we have always done for each other. I am thankful to have you both to walk with during moments in the valley, as well as on the mountaintop. Friendship doesn't cover what I have with you both. It never has and never will. I love you and thank you for being a part of my family.

I'd like to thank my nieces and nephews: every talk, every hug and every moment I am blessed to have. To be called your aunt, Aunt Banette or Nanny is one of my greatest joys. Never forget how much I love each of you.

And of course, to everyone who reads my book. Thank you from the bottom of my heart!

About the Author

Yvette lives in a small, quiet town nestled in Southwest Louisiana, with her husband, Lee. They have both worked for the same company for almost twenty years. In her spare time, she enjoys spending time with her family, working on handmade crafts, and of course writing. Her mother also loves to write and Yvette attributes her love for it, to her.

Diagnosed with Bi-polar one disorder in late 2010, Yvette started her journey of self-discovery and wellness, learning that medicine would only take her so far, and that she had to do the rest. She now considers herself to be living her dream, writing. This, "The Toolbox," is her first novel, but not her last. She is excited to share her world with you.

Also from

Rope Swing Publishing

Vickie's parents divorced when she was only nine years old, and it remains one of the toughest times of her life. As she shares parts of herself and other stories with you, she hopes you will better be prepared for how to handle divorce with your children.

"Please Don't Divorce Me" is candidly written as a parent's guide from a child's perspective for the benefit of the children, in hopes to salvage relationships and minimize hurt for what is already a difficult time in their life.

Divorce is not pretty, but it doesn't have to be ugly either. Choose children, love and happiness above all else!

"A tragic family saga."
Bookware History Blog

Passengers

ELIZABETH
COLLUMS

During the Great Irish Famine the Ewing family made
their way from their rural cottage to the village of
Highland Way. Annie, the oldest daughter, was left to
care for her mother and younger sister after her father
left to find work in Dublin.

A mysterious letter arrives from America forcing Annie,
Lily, and Katy into a harrowing journey. The hand
written note not only will expose deep secrets, it will
also challenge the strength and fortitude of the Ewing
women, leading each member into their own soul
searching voyage.

Follow this extraordinary passage that begins in
Ireland and leads each woman to uncover their own
courage and truths in this new world.

"Her writing is strong, truthful and addictive."
-Books are Love Blog Review

TWO THOUSAND LINES

MICHELLE JESTER

Olivia Brooks has been able to keep her life in Sugar Mill, Louisiana held perfectly together, far away from the small town where she grew up. Even though her past still haunts her, she has found a perfect process of surviving, until a string of events brings Luke Plaisance to Sugar Mill and turns her organized life upside down.

While Olivia fights to hold on to the life she's created, unraveling it may be exactly what it takes for her to truly survive. She must accept her past in order to live, or let it threaten the only future she's ever wanted. Because some secrets can't stay buried... and shouldn't.

An inspiring and heartbreaking tale of abandonment, survival, and purpose. A harrowing journey of self-discovery and perseverance.